Carshalton Hall

Carshalton Hall

A. Z. WRIGHT

LUTE PUBLISHING

This first edition published in 2017

1 3 5 7 9 10 8 6 4 2

ISBN 978-0-9931453-2-2

Typeset by Deltatype Ltd, Birkenhead, Merseyside
Printed in Great Britain by Biddles Books Ltd

for Lute Publishing

Contents

CHAPTER I

Thomas Pulleine, Esquire, of Carshalton Hall in the North Riding of Yorkshire and Justice of the Peace stared uninterruptedly at the man who stood before the bench. The solid, rugged appearance and unreliable expression said everything; there could be no doubt in the minds of the justices that the accusations made against him were accurate and true. The rogue continued to deny the charge of bastardy, as read out by the magistrate:

12th October 1711. George Alderson of Eskeleth in Arkengarthdale, by fair promises, persuaded Hannah Hawkins, his servant, to let him have carnal knowledge of her body in his stable, about the middle of January last, and again in the parlour of his house about three or four weeks later, and she was delivered of twin boys on 21 Sept last.

Thomas Pulleine was ninety-nine percent certain that this was the man responsible for his own daughter's present condition. Catherine Pulleine was seventeen years of age and still unmarried, despite two potential matches that he had contrived for her. Her mother was no longer living. Recently, however, it had been revealed to him through the servants that she was with child. She was presently confined to the grounds of Carshalton Hall, where she would remain throughout her term. The only persons living at Carshalton

I

apart from his daughter were his sister and a select group of servants. The Hall was surrounded by large woods as were many of the Yorkshire estates. Thomas Pulleine's attitude to poaching was well-known throughout the district and trespassers were infrequent. Carshalton Hall was of a modest size; Thomas Pulleine himself did not reside there. Accustomed to a far more elevated standard of living, he rented an infinitely grander residence from the Duke of Bolton, located some fifteen miles from Carshalton.

The thought currently uppermost in his mind was the possibility that George Alderson might already be legally married to his daughter. No amount of gentle persuasion had extorted this information from her, and unlike some men of his generation, he was not prepared to stoop to violence. Under no conceivable perception was George Alderson describable as landed gentry and Thomas Pulleine could detect a fortune hunter when he saw one. Not that there was land to be had; a strict settlement directed the Pulleine estate in default of surviving sons not to the daughters of Thomas Pulleine, but to his brother. But there were also the marriage prospects of his daughter to be considered; although sometimes he wondered if Catherine desired to die an old maid; two refusals were already excessive, in his opinion. Then there was the further issue of what was to be done with the bastard child if born alive.

Thomas Pulleine pronounced the maximum possible fine and maintenance allowable by law for the case in question. His influence in the county was such that he was not opposed by any of the other justices presiding. The scribe seated below the bench coughed nervously as he wrote down in Latin these particulars. George Alderson did not appear to react in any way at all. He stepped down from the dock.

2

There then followed orders to the keeper of the House of Correction at Thirsk and to the Constable of Guisborough; the Constable to convey an idle vagrant woman aged about 30, who pretends to be dumb and to tell fortunes by signs, to the House of Correction, who are ordered to receive her and put her to hard labour. After which one John Metcalfe, on refusal to provide for his ailing mother-in-law was fined and ordered to pay.

"You can wipe your backsides with the order," yelled the jaggedly countenanced miner, leaning towards the justices threateningly and defiantly from the dock. His remarks were duly noted by the scribe and justices alike.

The proceedings concluded well before dusk. Thomas Pulleine descended the stone steps of the Market Hall at Thirsk and walked quickly in his usual short, hurried step, across the market square, then turned into Finkle street, and stopped outside an alehouse halfway down by the name of Ye Olde Three Tuns. Raucous and boisterous sounds emanated from its drab interior. With only a moment's hesitation, he stepped inside. Glancing quickly around the smoky boozing den, he recognized with certainty the figures of George Alderson and John Metcalfe, seated at a corner table near the back wall. Both men had seen him enter, and were watching him with sarcastic expression. As the justice approached, John Metcalfe got up suddenly and strode over to him and would have struck him, had he not been immediately restrained by George Alderson, who came behind him and pulled him away, then towards the door. Thomas Pulleine informed George Alderson that he wished to speak with him alone. The latter persuaded John Metcalfe that they should part company; the aggrieved miner moved off discourteously with a grunt. In a secluded room at the

3

back of the alehouse, the conversation which ensued was conducted in calm, quiet tones.

"I am immune to scandal." Thomas Pulleine's voice was coarse, even had vestiges of the local dialect. "A man of my wealth does not need to concern himself with such a thing. And I may be able to help you. But first I would like some information."

George Alderson was happy to tell the justice that although nothing had been recorded and no priest had been present, at the last fair at Aldbrough St John two witnesses had heard both him and Catherine Pulleine utter the phrases, 'I do take thee to my wife,' and "I do take thee to my husband." However, since then one of the witnesses had died. The other was the lowliest of peasants. Only his word could nullify a future marriage of Catherine to another.

"I am prepared to pay for the fine and maintenance costs of the twins born by your maid," said Thomas Pulleine, in certain pronouncement. "However you must assure me that you will never bring the case to court that you are the husband of my daughter. Not that it would be a strong case. The word of a peasant is not highly regarded in our society."

A satisfied look crossed the heavy features of George Alderson. He took a swig of his beer.

"That would be an acceptable arrangement," he responded. "Though I fear that the truth may already be known in the district. The people of Arkengarthdale believe me to be married to your daughter."

"Gossip is no proof of marriage," said the justice. "It is of no concern to me."

"Then I shall not utter a word," said George Alderson. "You may depend on it. But what of your daughter's child? What shall become of it?"

"It shall be handed to a caretaker at birth," was the justice's reply.

"Caretakers are careless," stated George Alderson. "It may not survive, even if you were to keep up the payments."

"I shall endeavour to find someone reliable," said Thomas Pulleine. "I do not wish my grandchild to die in the hands of a careless caretaker."

"In that case, I may have an agreeable solution. I would like to adopt the child," said George Alderson in a tone of confidence. "That is if you were to pay the maintenance costs of that child as well as the others."

"You would bring it up as your own?"

"It is my own."

"I would not wish it to be known in the area that the child is the offspring of yourself and my daughter."

"It is already known. But as you say, village gossip has no legal bearing."

"I shall consider it."

"If you are happy to agree, I shall welcome the child into my own house as soon as it is born," said George Alderson. "If it is a boy, he shall take the name of George Alderson."

On an indifferent afternoon in Spring, late in the twentieth century, George Alderson, born 1st January 1964, was sitting in the Local History Section of York Public Library. Despite a lack of interest in his immediate relatives, he had felt compelled to uncover his ancestral past. In the London repositories, he had examined the Old Parish Records of Births, Marriages and Deaths and had discovered that his remote ancestor George Alderson alias Pulen of Eskeleth in Arkengarthdale had died in 1754 at the age of forty-two. That meant by George's calculations that he had been born in the year 1712. This was useful to know, for there were no Old Parish Records for Arkengarthdale prior to 1727, for what reason, George did not know. He had wondered about the name, 'Pulen'. Amongst the records, there were no people of that name in the area. But now, from further research in the York Library, it had now emerged that 'Pulen' was really 'Pulleine', spelt carelessly, as was done in the eighteenth century. As for the 'alias', he had been told that a very possible reason for this was illegitimacy. In other words, George Alderson alias Pulen had been a bastard. This idea pleased George. His other ancestors had all been so prim and proper. His pleasure was further enhanced on consulting the library catalogue; for according to this, the library held an old book that listed the pedigrees of Yorkshire families, including the pedigree of Pulleine. So it was possible that not only was his ancestor a bastard, he was also a blue-blooded bastard. That idea pleased George even more. He had requested to view the book and now could not wait for the librarian to bring it up from the bowels of the library when he was sure that all would be revealed.

The librarian, however, seemed to be taking a long time. This was no real problem for George, as he always had ample amounts of time, being unemployed. He had been unemployed for five years. The only drawback to this situation was that his income was limited. He did, however, top up his incapacity benefit with winnings incurred by the occasional game of poker. He had thought of playing on a more professional level somewhere abroad but had realised that such a project would involve as much work as any other job, and was therefore not worth it. But if there was a game taking place at the back of a Greek or Portuguese restaurant, there was nothing to stop him joining in and winning more than enough for a few good restaurant meals. It was certainly a more cheerful way to spend an evening than watching videos or brooding over Anne in his cramped, shabby and dilapidated council flat in South London. Anne was his 'girlfriend', as he chose to call her, but he had not seen her for over a year. No one in the world was as attractive as Anne; she had an indefinable quality that made him feel useful if only she would let him be so. The potential for a strong relationship was there.

George wandered over to the catalogue drawers again. Perhaps it might be an idea to look up Carshalton Hall, the seat of the Pulleines. There was one entry: Carshalton Hall was featured extensively in an issue of a magazine published in 1900. George saw the librarian finally approaching him, carrying a wide, battered book bound in blue vellum.

"I've got dust on my hands, now," she complained, handing it to him. George did not care. "I'm sorry to send you back down again, but could you fetch this as well?" he asked politely, indicating the catalogue entry. She observed it dutifully.

"Yes."

Well, she needs to do something to keep fit, thought George. He went back and sat down again with the book of pedigrees. It was arranged alphabetically. The Pedigree of Pulleine, of Carshalton Hall, was displayed longways over a page near the centre of the book. George viewed enviously the coat of arms, positioned at the left of the tree. Below it, in pompous explanation, was written,

'ARMS: Az, a bend cottised arg., charged with three escallops gu., on a chief or three martlets of the field. CREST: A pelican feeding its young, all or.' He was awed by such unfamiliar jargon. The tree itself was no less impressive. Which of its members could be a parent of George Alderson alias Pulen, born 1712? Perhaps one of the children of Thomas Pulleine Esquire, High Sheriff of York in 1696 and 1703. He avidly viewed the entries.

Thomas Pulleine, died young.

Wingate Pulleine, died August 1763, buried at St. John's, Stanwick. Married Frances, daughter of Ralph Carr, Esq. of Cocken Hall, County Durham. He succeeded Thomas Pulleine.

Dorothy Pulleine, married to Reginald Marriott., Esq., M.P. for Weymouth.

Catherine.

Mary Pulleine, married to Richard Garth, Esq., of Morden, co. Surrey.

Frances, died young.

Any one of them could conceivably be a parent of George Alderson alias Pulen. But which was the correct one? Possibly not Mary or Dorothy, as both had married well. Frances and Thomas had died young, that presumably meant before adulthood. That left only Wingate and Catherine. Wingate had married and succeeded his father. George wondered why no information was given concerning Catherine. If she had not married, died young, or died unmarried, what had she done? Surely from a logical viewpoint, she must have done one of those things. At this moment, the librarian returned with an enormous, dusty black volume.

"I'm sorry to keep making you run up and down," said George. "I'd go myself if it was allowed."

"Don't worry, I need the exercise." George was already searching for the issue. Within this issue, an ornate banner ran across the top:

COUNTRY HOMES   GARDENS OLD AND NEW
CARSHALTON, YORKSHIRE
The Seat of Henry Percy Pulleine

His eyes fell upon the photograph of Carshalton Hall. It consisted of an old building to which was asymmetrically attached a Georgian East Wing with a higher roof. Ivy spread copiously over the façade of the older building. To George it looked slightly bizarre, but he was not complaining. It was certainly a far cry from his dilapidated council flat. In front of the Hall, a gravelled path surrounded a large, well-kept lawn, over which a giant oak tree spread its branches. George became overwhelmed with desire to visit the place. He began reading the text:

'Carshalton Hall is completely surrounded by large woods but can be accessed by avenues therein. There is a lack of sign-posting, and for the stranger, it is difficult to find. A field behind the Hall runs

9

down to the beck beyond which are meadows and woodland. To the north lies an orchard. There is also an ice-house at Carshalton.'

George felt increasingly drawn to Carshalton Hall. He would have much preferred to live there than in his present accommodation. It seemed like such an idyllic existence; not to have to worry about bills or incapacity benefit review forms. Fate alone had put him in the council flat and the Pulleines in Carshalton Hall. He turned the page and was confronted by a second photograph depicting the church of Stanwick-St-John, purported by the article to be the burial place of all Pulleines. He read the text below:

'From the gate at Carshalton Lodge runs a private road to the mediaeval church of Stanwick-St-John, built c 1200, but heavily restored in 1868 for the Duchess of Northumberland by Anthony Salvin. Most of its windows are of that date, but one south aisle east window dates from the late 13th century. The porch pillars, tower and part of the chancel remain much the same.'

The article appeared to be drifting. It talked of the many archaeological remains to be found in the surrounding countryside. George stopped reading. His thoughts returned to the question of his possible ancestral link to the Pulleines. Presumably, the tree given in the Pedigree Families of North Yorkshire was not comprehensive. Perhaps George Alderson alias Pulen had descended from a minor line of the Pulleines. Or perhaps he did not descend from them at all, for the term alias did not always refer to illegitimacy. However, George was already involuntarily forming a plan to visit Carshalton and see for himself the great house that he was already regarding as his legacy.

Catherine Pulleine was not permitted to leave the grounds of Carshalton Hall. She had no great desire to do so. She was in no condition for horse riding and had never found good company at the few social events in the area that she had graced with her presence. She felt safe within the seclusion of the Hall. A dense thicket surrounded it, and Catherine had the suspicion that her father had placed man-traps at strategic points throughout it, as well as employing a couple of potentially murderous groundsmen. She had seen them in the hallway, in discourse with her father, on his occasional visits to the Hall. They spoke in rough, local accents and had a rugged, purple countenance. She was reclining on the Turkish divan in a room beautifully decorated with a new and expensive blue wallpaper on the upper floor of the Hall, reading, "The Storm", by a modern writer by the name of Daniel Defoe. She did not really enjoy reading. Nobody appeared to write the sort of books that she would want to read. She laid aside the book and rose awkwardly to her feet. It was getting harder to enjoy a normal existence. At least it was only a temporary situation that she suffered. In two months time, everything would be as before. Then in a few more years, she would leave Carshalton Hall. Not to get married, but to go to London. She would travel by sea. She knew that there were big ships sailing every week from Hull, which carried passengers as well as cargo; a far more attractive option than the cramped coach from York, in which you never knew who would be sitting beside you, or in front of you. The question now was, what to do in the meantime. Four more years of lying on the divan, trying to read uninteresting books. It could be borne. She gazed through the large, latticed windows, into the field running down to the beck at the back of the house. Last year the beck had completely frozen over, but now the water still ran. Her mind began to wander. She was wearing the loose gown of a heavy material dyed in the same deep purple as the riding habit in which Richardson had painted her, not a year ago. Richardson had been old but still had long, sensitive fingers. Then there had been her clavichord teacher, Paolo, charming and handsome in a swarthy way, but Catherine had seen through him. He really wasn't a very good clavichord player, either, she had concluded. In fact, she had suspected that he wasn't a clavichord player at all, but a violinist. He had provided her with transcriptions of violin pieces by Corelli to practice and even boasted that he knew the man. After a while, the clavichord lessons had fizzled out. As for George Alderson, Catherine Pulleine had never seen him again. She was beginning to forget what he looked like. At least she was no longer forced to attend church.

It was approaching four of the clock. She decided to take a turn around the field by the beck until the commencement of dinner. But as she drifted down the oak staircase she was met by her aunt, who insisted that the cold December air would be detrimental to her condition. She returned instead to the library, in despondent mood.

CHAPTER 2

It was the second week of May 1994. George Alderson was on a train from London King's Cross to Darlington, from where he would go on to the village of Aldbrough-St-John. It had been an uncomfortable two and a half hours, crammed in the toilets for much of the journey, but that was how he was accustomed to travelling by rail. Some distance from the station, he boarded a bus and was soon jaunting through the North Yorkshire countryside. He gazed out of the windows and reflected on his mission. What relics of the Pulleine pedigree still lay in the manor? George had not really formulated a plan. He was beginning to realize that it was unlikely that the current Pulleines would receive him. However, the idea of seeing Carshalton Hall with his own eyes excited him no end.

At twenty-five past one the bus drove into Aldbrough-St-John and deposited him at the bus shelter on the village green. Ahead in front of him was a house with a red sign attached displaying the words, 'The Stanwick Arms'. A quick drink would not do him any harm, and the landlord might give him useful information. George crossed the grass and walked in through the white-framed, glass doors of the premises, expecting to be greeted by a shocked silence from the locals. Instead, he was largely ignored. There were not many people there, and those that were, were not of an urban walk of life, but none-the-less appeared perfectly normal. George walked over to the bar. There was nobody serving, and he had to ring a bell to receive attention. Finally, the proprietor appeared. George ordered a pint of Stella Artois. As he placed the coins on the counter, he ventured,

"Do you know of a place called Carshalton?"

"Oh, yes."

"Could you give me directions?" George had not been bothered to consult an ordnance survey map. He normally preferred to rely on geographical information given to him on reaching the local area.

"Well, you go over the old stone bridge, past the church, turn right along the main road and eventually you'll get there. Are you walking?"

"Yes."

"Well, it's about a mile and a half."

"Thank you." Then he added, "Who lives at Carshalton, now?"

The proprietor took the change that George had placed upon the bar counter.

"The Pulleines," he answered readily, but not volunteering any more information. George felt awkward. He went and sat down at the window with his drink and stared out at the deserted green. Aldbrough really was a very quiet place. He was glad he did not live there. Hopefully Carshalton would be better.

Ten minutes later, George left the pub and walked off along the main road. He crossed the stone bridge over the babbling beck, and then noticed a gate on the right, with a yellow arrow painted on one side. In the distance he saw the main road outlined by a hedge, running along the far side of the fields. It looked a bit of a trek. Perhaps the footpath over the fields would be quicker. George immediately climbed over the gate and ambled off along the dirt track, alongside the beck. The air was still quite cool, despite it being May. Eventually he came to another gate, with another yellow arrow, and still keeping the main road in view, climbed over that as well. Now he was wading through thick wet grass, and the landscape opened up beyond into distant fields and meadows, beneath a clouding sky. Up ahead was dense woodland. As it was the only one in sight, George assumed that this was Carshalton Wood.

Carshalton Hall, he knew, lay somewhere within it. The wind rustled through the trees and a wood pigeon called, as George stood hesitantly at the start of an avenue leading inwards. A large sign with the word PRIVATE at the side of the path faced him menacingly. As he took the first step, he began hoping that he would not be shot by a gamekeeper or caught in a man trap. It was quite idyllic within the wood. There were bluebells everywhere, amongst green, leafy plants; the sound of the nearby beck mingled with the wind. He progressed inwards. However, after about one hundred yards, the avenue petered out. He had got the wrong avenue. As made his way back along the path, he remembered what it had said in the magazine about the Hall being difficult to find. That was the idea, he supposed.

When he did find the Hall, it was by accident. He suddenly emerged from the trees into the wide gravelled area in front of Carshalton Hall. It looked exactly the same as in the photograph. For a while, he stood and stared quietly at the building.

At this moment Lady Pulleine was seated in the morning room on the ground floor of the East Wing, darning. The activity was a pleasure to her and something that she never bothered the servants with. Although at one time there had been over one hundred employees on the estate, now there were but five: a cook, two housemaids, a gardener and a handyman. The cook and one of the housemaids lived at the Hall and were company for her, along with what she regarded as her gormless son. Becoming of late somewhat less mobile than before, she rarely ventured upstairs, and hardly ever crossed the threshold of the West Wing which constituted the old part of the Hall. This had been seriously neglected for many decades. It was almost as it was that day early in the century when most of the furniture was removed from it and transferred to the East Wing. All around the landing on the first floor of the West Wing were portraits of Pulleine ancestors of her long-since dead husband. The really old portraits, however, were in the Gallery. It was there that the painting of a seventeen-year-old Catherine Pulleine still hung, but unnamed, amidst other paintings of near and distant relations. Lady Pulleine looked up from her darning and peered over her half-rimmed glasses through the latticed windows into the distance. She thought she could make out a man walking around at the edge of the woods, observing the Hall. Trespassers were not unknown. The most annoying ones were those who chose to picnic in the 'Grotto'. She did not feel particularly alarmed, for both Gertrude and her son were at home. Expecting the man to go away very soon, she focused on her darning again. But on realising ten minutes later that he was still there, she decided to send Gertrude out to find out who it was.

On seeing Gertrude approaching him, George hesitated. He felt that he should walk away, but felt rooted to the spot.

"Would you be wanting anything, sir?" called out Gertrude, as she came up to him. It was a bit windy, and her dyed hair waved about her ever young face.

"Er, yes, possibly," said George, awkwardly. He did not know how to put it. Finally, he said,

"I am researching my family history, and wish to photograph the Hall. I believe they lived here."

"Oh," said Gertrude. There was a pause. "Well, Lady Pulleine doesn't like uninvited visitors on the estate. We have too many of them." Feeling increasingly uncomfortable, George decided to leave. "I'm sorry to have troubled you," he said. He was about to turn away, then remembered about the private road to the church. "I don't suppose you could direct me to Stanwick Church, could you?"

"Through there," indicated the maid, uncertainly. Someway to the left of the Hall, George could see a gabled outhouse. That must be Carshalton Lodge, he told himself. Through an open gate, a path led into the woodland again.

"Thank you very much," said George. The maid stared at him dubiously as he disappeared into the trees. Then she walked back over the gravel, shivering slightly. She came back into the morning-room.

"I see he's gone now," said Lady Pulleine, looking up as she walked in.

"Yes. It was a bit odd. Said his ancestors used to live here."

"Did he want to see anything in particular?"

"He said something about photographing the Hall. Then he just walked off again, towards the church."

"Well, as long as he wasn't a dangerous man," concluded Lady Pulleine.

Presumably, thought George, the private road was the means by which vehicles accessed the Hall. It cut through the forest with a line of grass growing down the middle. Perhaps this path had always existed. Perhaps Catherine Pulleine had walked along it, dressed in the gear of the day. As he ambled along between the trees, he half expected to meet her, or her ghost. Just before the road left the woods, it forked; George took the lesser path which lead out into a flat plain of thick, dark green grass. Carshalton Wood fell away behind him. The square tower of the mediaeval church of Stanwick-St-John rose up before him. The accumulating clouds were now a bluish grey. As he came ever closer, he could see that the churchyard was encircled by yew trees and a low stone wall. A herd of black and white cows grazed in the field before him, beside watery blue pools.

Finally he reached the encircling wall and climbed up two iron handles fastened into it. Around him, all facing west, the sunken gravestones lay. Some were worn away and leaning; a few were shiny and new. George walked slowly around the old stone walls of the church. Along one, where a rose bush grew, he found tombstones of several of the Pulleines. The most prominent was that of Henry Percy Pulleine, on whose no expense had been spared. Next to him on either side were Winifred Pulleine and James Pulleine. They all lay in a row together, from one buttress to the next. However, at the end, a space still remained, as though awaiting a missing Pulleine. A slight shiver ran through George and he walked on. When he came round to the front of the church again, he was standing in front of a wire gate in the archway entrance. He stepped through into a kind of stone porch way where an old, wooden door was set, with black metal fastenings. George turned the black metal circular handle and pushed the heavy door slowly forwards. A thick red velvet curtain hung in front of him. George lifted it aside.

He was now standing inside the dark and quiet church. The air was musty, and he appeared to be alone. Wandering down the aisle, he observed the hatchments high up on the wall above the pews. In the poor light, George could just about make out that one of them was a memorial to Wingate Pulleine. He came up closer to observe it. Underneath the main inscription were more names, but these were illegible.

Near the altar was a row of high-backed pews, which ran along one after the other, like railway compartments. George opened the door of the nearest one and stepped in. At the back, fastened in brass, was the familiar crest of the Pulleines, depicting a pelican feeding its young. George sat himself down upon the wooden seat. It was rather uncomfortable; you had to put your feet up on a sort of ledge at the bottom of the door. He stood up again and stepped out, whereupon he was confronted by the sight of a tall, slim young man of about twenty with an amiable countenance, standing by the altar. He had, thought George, an air of one too nice for his own good and easily led. George felt startled and confused but then recovered himself. He surmised that the man might be in some way connected with Carshalton Hall.

"Don't worry, it's not a private church," said the young man, in a light hearted voice.

"I know," said George. The young man stood expectantly, with a continual smile, not embarrassed, but at a loss. George felt that he should say something.

"Do you live at Carshalton Hall?" he asked.

"Yes, I do. Is there anything that I can help you with?"

George began to realise that the guy must have seen him from the house and followed him along the private road towards the church. He felt slightly uncomfortable.

"Well, yes, there might be," he said. He walked out into the nave and up to the altar, where he began to relate the details of his genealogical research and the possibility that he was descended from the Pulleines. In particular that he might be descended from Catherine or Wingate Pulleine. As he spoke, the young man did not take his eyes off him; he seemed to be regarding him in a bewitched manner that George found rather disturbing. However he was prepared to put up with it, should the man be of use to him in some form.

"I'm George, by the way," he said, and smiled.

The young man seemed delighted to be properly introduced. "And I'm Ralph. Ralph Pulleine. Well, I've no idea if you are related to the Pulleines. I suppose you've seen the memorial to Wingate Pulleine, up on the north wall," he said. "There are also a lot of illegible names carved low down on it, but a ladder would be needed to decipher them. Also, I can tell you, some of the Pulleines are buried underneath this church, by the north wall, where their hatchment is."

"Wouldn't they have to take up a pew to do that?" asked George.

"Yes, but the church was rebuilt about a hundred and fifty years ago, by the Duchess of Northumberland. After that, the Pulleines were buried in their own special plot, outside."

"Yes, I saw it," said George.

There was an awkward silence, which George eventually broke.

"Well," he said. "I suppose I'd better be getting back to Aldbrough. My bus leaves at four."

"Are you walking?" Ralph seemed disappointed, very disappointed.

"Yes."

"I'd offer you a lift, but I don't have a car," said Ralph.

"How on earth do you get around?" asked George.

"I walk. Sometimes I bicycle, but that's a bit dangerous."

"Wouldn't it be easier to drive?"

Ralph looked embarrassed. "I can't drive," he said.

Ralph did not appear to be a completely normal person. What on earth did he do all day, stuck up at Carshalton Hall? He must be as lonely as anything.

"Would you like to go for a drink down at Aldbrough, Ralph?" asked George. An elated expression appeared upon Ralph's face.

"Well, yes, I would, but The Stanwick Arms is closed until six. We could go then, if you like. But your bus . . .

I'll tell you what, George, why don't you come back to the house for a drink?"

"I'd love to, Ralph," said George.

At five of the clock in the morning of February 1712, Catherine Pulleine was pacing the floorboards of her bedchamber at Carshalton Hall. She was presently living alone with the servants, for her aunt had departed some four days ago to attend to a woman afflicted by a fever, and had still not returned. A strong chill had enveloped the room during the night to which she was not acclimatised. A shiver had taken over her body. She went over to the window and held her hand out at the bottom of the frame to feel a freezing current of air rushing in. Outside, in an absence of snow, the ground was hard. In the diminishing darkness, the oak tree at the far end of the lawn and the woods in the background were bare and barren.

Catherine walked through the adjoining room and out onto the landing. Tentatively taking the first two steps up the wooden staircase towards the uppermost level of the Hall, she called out to Hippolyta to light a fire in her room. There was no response. She walked up a further two steps and called again. Finally, a door was heard to creak open on the upper corridor, and Hippolyta's Yorkshire tones resounded down to her from above.

"Do it yourself, you common hussy, for I'll not rise before six of the clock."

The door slammed shut. Catherine walked back down the stairs again. Once returned to her bedchamber, she sat upon the embroidered covers, enveloping herself in them. She would wait for the fire to be lit. But within half-an-hour,

a pain of indescribable acuteness suddenly afflicted her, and
her subsequent cries brought servants to her room.

As George and Ralph approached the black and gleaming front door to the East Wing of the Hall, Gertrude was on her knees, polishing the door furniture. She looked up at them with a troubled curiosity. "Oh, you're back, sir," she said to Ralph, as they came up to her, stopping momentarily. "This is George," said Ralph, as though he had just made a marvellous discovery. "He's come to have a look around the house."

"Oh. Right you are, sir."

"Step this way, George," said Ralph, proudly and invitingly. George followed his host into a dimly lit entrance hallway.

He was finally standing inside Carshalton Hall. All around the upper walls, stuffed animal heads with gigantic antlers and staring eyes leaned outwards. A gun rack stacked with rifles stood beside the staircase, and two sturdy looking oak chairs of an antique appearance flanked a large open fireplace.

"I suppose the West Wing would be the most interesting part of the house," said Ralph, who appeared pleased and elated to have a visitor. "It is a hundred years older than the East Wing, in which we are now standing."

"I would be very interested to see the West Wing," said George, sincerely.

"Well, come along and I'll show you," said Ralph, immediately, leading the way towards the next room. "That's where mother lives," he added, as they passed a door on the left. "She has a suite of rooms in there."

"I suppose the Hall is too big for her," said George.

"Oh, yes. But that's where she retreats to. It's her sanctuary."

"She'd be better off in a little cottage somewhere," said George.

"Maybe. But she has no plans to leave."

They had arrived at a large, portentous looking door set in the west wall of the East Wing. Like the chairs in the hallway, it was ornately carved from oak.

"I warn you, it's a bit dusty in here," said Ralph. "Nobody's been in here much for almost a century."

Ralph pushed at the heavy door which creaked ominously as it opened. They stepped over a wooden threshold into a musty, empty room with wide, high walls painted in a turquoise blue. Standing in the light, open space, George gazed around admiringly at the chipped areas of gold dotted around the doors and ceilings. Brass candlesticks still remained screwed to the crumbling plasterwork, and an obvious blank rectangle occupied a space above a disused fireplace.

"This would have been the Blue Drawing-room," explained Ralph. "But as you see, the furniture is no longer here. It was all removed to the East Wing a long time ago."

George glanced at Ralph. "It's certainly not claustrophobic," he enthused.

"No," agreed Ralph. "Though most of the other rooms are a bit smaller."

He walked on towards a door near the fireplace and opened it. It led into a sombre hallway where a dark, oak staircase which scrolled round at the bottom lead upstairs.

"Was it portraits that you wanted to see, George?"

asked Ralph. George had mentioned portraits on the walk back along the private road.

"Portraits would be extremely interesting," said George. "Though I don't suppose they will all be looking like me."

Ralph smiled. "I believe we do have some eighteenth century portraits of the Pulleines," he said. "Up in the Gallery, I am sure there are some, and also on the landing." He seemed amazingly anxious to help. George followed the young man up the first flight of steps. Within a wall recess stood a dusty white porcelain statuette of a nude cherub. That must be worth a bob or two, thought George. In his extremely inexpert opinion, it was either Greek or Italian. He wondered for how many decades it had been there. When they reached the landing, the melancholy faces of eighteenth century women stared out at them. All appeared to George to be vain, or simple-minded, or miserable.

"I think these are mid-eighteenth century," commented Ralph. "That one is my great-great-great-great-great-grandmother."

"Oh," said George. Ralph looked at him.

"But the ones in the Gallery are older."

George followed Ralph through a doorway off the landing into a spacious room decorated by a peeling and faded wallpaper. An L-shaped divan with a white balustrade at each end furnished one corner of the room and a large, scratched mirror with an intricately shaped gilded frame on the wall opposite the latticed windows reflected the beck and woodlands outside. Other than this the room was empty. "This was the Divan Room," informed Ralph, without stopping. "The Gallery is just along here," he said, leading on through an empty room with a high ceiling and decorated with beige plasterwork. They passed through another landing at the top of a bare secondary staircase. Finally Ralph stopped in the middle of a square room lined with old oak panelling. One wall was almost entirely covered by a gigantic tapestry hanging on a very long metal rod. The colours had lost their vibrancy, but it appeared to be some kind of outdoor scene with horses and woodlands. On the wall opposite in diagonal array was a group of dull, expressionless portraits. Below this, on an antique table, a bemused barn owl, stuffed centuries ago, was encased in a glass cover.

"This is the Gallery," said Ralph.

George had thought that a Gallery was a long, narrow room in which you could walk up and down. He had been a little surprised when Ralph had claimed that Carshalton Hall possessed one.

"It's a nice room, Ralph," he said.

"Yes," said Ralph. "And I believe that these portraits are early eighteenth century."

The portraits were extremely faded and dusty. A couple of them were torn in places. Some were men, some were women, yet their faces all looked much the same: blank, pallid and a little superior. All except the one of a young girl in purple riding dress trimmed with silver, seated on a chestnut-coloured mare. In the far background of the painting was Carshalton Wood. Beyond a field rose the tower of Stanwick Church. Ash blonde hair beneath a tall, felt hat with a feather flowed copiously around a plain looking face. The eyes, of a green-grey tint, were alive and arresting. Perhaps, thought George wishfully, this is Catherine Pulleine. Even Anne seemed to pale in the presence of this interesting and attractive woman. George started. He had not thought of Anne all day.

"It's a shame they aren't named and dated," he said, turning to Ralph. "It's guesswork, determining who they all are."

"Not entirely. That one is definitely Wingate Pulleine, who succeeded Thomas Pulleine in 1726. You were asking about him, weren't you?"

"Yes," said George. For some reason, he had expected Wingate Pulleine to be tall and slim. Instead, he was short and fat. What was more, he was blonde.

There was a pause. Ralph coughed.

"Would you like to see the rest of the house?" he asked, politely.

"Well, I would like to see the library," said George. "Especially if you have any old books or documents."

"Oh, yes, plenty. But most of them pertain to mining."

Ralph went back out of the Gallery and led the way into a dark, green room, with heavy green curtains, a four-poster bed and green wallpaper.

"This is a Victorian en-suite guestroom," said Ralph. He opened a dark wooden door to reveal a nineteenth century porcelain sink and lavatory with wood furnishings, a mirror and gold taps. "The plumbing's not working now," he said, allowing George to look inside. They then came through a wide double-door, which lead into the adjoining room. This room was far lighter, as no curtains adorned the high windows. A harpsichord, or possibly a clavichord, stood close to one wall, indicating it to be some kind of music room. By one window stood a harp. Ralph walked over to the other window and pushed up the lower frame. Voices were audible from the ground below. George came over to Ralph and looked out. A short lawn led into a field and down to the beck. A woman with grey hair and of advanced middle age was sitting at a garden table near the back of the house, about to be served tea by the maid. Ralph called out to her, addressing her as 'mother'. The woman turned her head towards the window.

"I'm coming down to have tea with you," said Ralph, loudly. "I've got a visitor."

A couple of minutes later they were walking across the short grass towards the mother. As they reached her, she looked up at George in an irritated and displeased manner.

"This is George," said Ralph.

"You were here earlier," said the mother. "I believe you wanted to photograph the Hall."

"I did, but didn't want to impose."

"Well, you are certainly imposing now."

There was an awkward silence.

"I'd better go," said George.

"You'll do no such thing," interrupted Ralph. "Sit down and have some tea."

George hesitated, then obeyed, taking the seat furthest from the mother.

"George is a Pulleine descendant," began Ralph, in an upbeat tone.

The mother did not respond. Ralph began to explain to her the possible significance of the Pulleine alias, to which she listened without a smile. George filled in with the details. The mother appeared singularly unimpressed. Finally she turned to George but did not really look at him.

"I'm not saying that you could not be a Pulleine descendant," she said. "I'm just saying that there are more likely possibilities."

"Such as?"

"Such as your ... Alderton ancestor may have worked for the Pulleines. You said that he was a lead miner."

"Mining agent."

"Yes, well anyway, I think that is a much more likely explanation," the mother concluded in a final tone. As that appeared to be the end of the matter, neither George nor Ralph spoke.

"George would like to do some research in the Old Library," said Ralph, finally. The mother did not respond.

"If that is agreeable to you," he added.

"This is your house, Ralph," said the mother.

"I'm sorry to trouble you," said George to the mother, politely.

"You've never been sorry in your life."

Ralph got up. "Come back to the house, George," he said.

George was glad to escape from the mother. Hopefully he would not be seeing much of her. A strong and peculiar feeling of discomfort invoked by the interaction was afflicting him. Would it persist or would it soon wear off? In any other circumstances, he would have put the woman in her place. But he had considered his current situation to be vulnerable and had said nothing. Now he was all the more determined to find evidence or proof of his descent from the Pulleines. The Old Library stretched across the west wall of the West Wing. Long, wooden shelves aligned either side of the narrow room, stacked from floor to ceiling with numerous dusty volumes. It was dark, and the air was stifling, but Ralph pulled back all the curtains and raised the sash windows. George was a little afraid that he might be outstaying his welcome. But far from being on the verge of sending George on his merry way, Ralph went down to the cellar and brought up two bottles of beer for further sustenance. George was sitting on the dark, narrow floorboards, sifting through various letters, but all were dated from the nineteenth century. Many were written to Henry Percy Pulleine, concerning a financial transaction of some description and did not touch on domestic matters. He suddenly became aware that Ralph was hovering. "Can I help at all, George?" the young man asked. George looked up. His polite state was starting to wear off.

"Well, yes. I'm looking for anything to do with Wingate or Catherine Pulleine."

"You haven't found anything, yet?"

"No, you're right, it is all business letters."

To George's dismay, Ralph squatted down on the floor beside him.

"Let's see," he said and began to sift through the faded, yellowed papers.

"This one's to Henry Percy Pulleine, from the Duke of Northumberland."

"Yes."

'After getting up and pretending to leave several times, he finally agreed upon the price of ...' read out Ralph. "It's not really relevant." Ralph glanced at George. "No eighteenth century letters, then?"

"Not that I can see. Not in this box, anyway."

"Oh. I don't think there are any other boxes of letters,

George. You're definitely sure it's either Wingate or Catherine you're descended from?"

"Yes," replied George. He was far from sure, but it seemed like a good idea to appear confident about his connections with the Pulleine family.

"Well, there's still all the books."

"Where are the oldest books?"

Ralph crossed his legs. "I think they're just scattered about. Gosh, it's dusty in here."

"Well, I'll just go through them systematically."

George scrambled to his feet. Ralph was making him feel uncomfortable again. Ralph remained on the floor, as he sifted through the heaviest, dustiest books on the lowest planks of the oak shelves that circumvented the room.

Ralph started to rabbit on.

"I haven't been in here for a while. In fact, hardly anybody has been in here for a while."

"A while? Like about a hundred years."

"Yes, possibly. It's such a job keeping a place up."

George tried not to look at Ralph, lest he should see the absolute contempt in which he now held him. If I were Lord of the Manor, thought George, I would have spent a fortune on the place, restoring it to its former, eighteenth century glory. The search for his ancestry appeared to be futile. There were some old mining books, from the early eighteenth century, however, and in one was folded an old letter from a John Alderson to Henry Percy Pulleine, dated 1826 in black ink in the top left-hand corner of the paper.

'Honred Sir,' the letter began, in faded ornate writing. 'I have sent you an account of what the old writings specifyes concerning the working of Taylors Rigg ...'

It was another useless letter. Though it did show that there were papers concealed in some of the books. He would have to search them all. George glanced at his watch. It was already a quarter to six. He had definitely missed all the buses. The sun would be setting soon. As if reading his thoughts, Ralph suddenly piped up.

"Would you like to stay for dinner, George?"

George smiled at him warmly. "I'd love to Ralph," he said.

There were complications at the birth and fears that Catherine Pulleine would not survive. The doctor who was summoned was unable to reply with a certainty of mind whether or not the child would be born alive, or the mother remain so. He was compelled to dose heavily with ergot; ultimately a living boy was born, who was at once whisked away. There then followed an hour's respite from anxiety, after which Catherine died sleeping. "She would not have been unmarriable," said Thomas Pulleine. "At least, no more than before." But no one was still in the bedchamber to hear. The doctor had collected his fee and departed sharply, glad at least to have delivered a healthy child, and not wishing to engage in any lengthy discourse concerning the cause of death of the mother.

CHAPTER 3

George had brought nothing to wear for dinner. Never in his wildest dreams had he envisaged dining at Carshalton Hall. Ralph had provided him with various items of clothing, possibly taken from his own dead father's wardrobe. They fitted him reasonably well. George was usually able to wear most things and remain presentable. He was pleased to use the en-suite bathroom with its generously provided towels, soaps and shampoos. George noted with satisfaction the gold taps and ornate marble floor. It was like residing in a five-star hotel. Back in the bedroom, he regarded himself in the wardrobe mirror. He could do with a shave. Never mind, he probably looked more rakish that way.

Now tolerably dressed, he descended the wide, shallow stairs upon which a red carpet was fastened by metal rods. The dining room was on the left. What had originally been a large room was now partitioned by a white, wooden wall with a door set in the middle. In the centre of the dining room was a circular table laid for two with expensive looking crockery and wine glasses. Ralph was there waiting for him and smiled happily as he entered. He asked George to sit down. The mother was not present; George did not ask why. Another maid, younger and whom George had not seen before, came through a swing door pushing a trolley laden with some concoction. He remained standing as she wheeled it over to the table.

"Do you just work here in the evenings?" George asked the maid.

"Oh, no sir. I'm a chamber maid, really," she answered in a local accent.

"How long have you worked here?"

She seemed surprised at his interest.

"Oh, I haven't worked here long, but my family has worked here for generations. My father's the gardener here."

"Oh, that's interesting."

"Sit down, George," invited Ralph, for the second time.

George sat down, removed the rolled up ironed linen napkin from its silver holder and placed it on his lap. He waited as the maid placed some kind of hors d'oeuvre and small plates upon the table. Outside, a dusk chorus could be heard. The maid went out through the swing door again, with the trolley. Through the French windows, the sun began to set behind the trees. A lovely, peaceful atmosphere pervaded the room. George opened the bottle of wine as Ralph did not seem entirely confident handling it. It was a very good wine.

"Have you ever been abroad, Ralph?" asked George, as they ate.

"No, apart from a day trip to Calais."

"Why not?"

"Well, for one thing, I'm terrified of flying. The thought of the plane taking off scares me half to death.

So I could only travel as far a Europe, I think. I get sea-sick as well. I'm not really that interested. I wouldn't travel well, I don't think. Also, I'm very fussy about what I eat."

"Well, have you ever been out of Yorkshire?"

"Yes, often. I went to school in Durham."

"A private boarding school?"

"Yes."

"They must have given you Hell." As he said this, George realized that it was perhaps not the right thing to say.

"They wouldn't go near me," answered Ralph quietly, after a pause.

A little later, the maid came in to collect the plates again. She began setting out the next course. It all looked most professional.

"You seem to live very well, Ralph," said George, when she had gone again, as he helped himself to the various platters laid out upon the table. "Not like some of us."

"Do I? I've never really thought about it. I've never known anything but here."

"Just as well," said George.

When the main course appeared to be over, there was a pause in the conversation. George could not think of anything appropriate to say.

"I'll go and see if the desert is ready," said Ralph finally.

He walked quickly out through the swing door. George looked around him at the surrounding décor and ornaments. He still wasn't clear exactly who owned what at

Carshalton Hall. If that mother of his was in possession of everything, it could be a while before Ralph inherited. She looked quite old, but if she was Ralph's mother, she had to be under seventy. On the mantelpiece stood an antique French clock. George knew that it was French because he had seen one just like it in the Victoria and Albert Museum in London. The time was now a quarter to nine. Presumably after the desert, there would be coffee and liqueurs. Then perhaps a heartfelt conversation during which Ralph would bare his soul, although George had absolutely no intention of baring his. He waited for Ralph to reappear through the swing doors. When he finally did so, he was carrying what looked like some kind of oven-baked pie.

"Careful, it's hot," warned Ralph, placing it carefully down on the table.

"Have you ever been to London, Ralph?" asked George, politely.

"Yes, once, on a day trip. I was about fourteen at the time. I visited all the museums."

"What, like the British Museum, and the National Gallery?"

"The Victoria and Albert Museum. That's the only one I really remember."

"What was special about it?"

"Well, I liked the gigantic statues in one of the rooms."

"What, Greek and Italian, you mean?"

"Yes, I think so. And I particularly liked a poem that was carved on the base of one of them. One of the verses stuck in my mind. It went something like:

All my life coldly and sadly
The days have gone by.
I who dreamed wildly and madly
Am happy to die.

There was a silence. George took a sip of wine.

"Have your days gone by coldly and sadly, Ralph?"

"Yes, they have. And I have also dreamed wildly and madly. I'm so glad you're here, George."

George laughed insincerely. "I'm glad to be here too, Ralph," he said and took another sip of wine.

Catherine did not lie there long. Once her earthly body had been taken from the room, the aunt returned. She ordered Hippolyta to swab the floor and windows and to put clean sheets upon the bed. Hipployta was then left alone.

A little later, the maid was awkwardly carrying an iron pail of water up the servants' staircase, being careful not to spill. Once returned to Catherine's bedchamber, she set down with relief the bucket and mop. She opened the windows. With a rag, she dusted the walnut dresser and mirror. Then after a moment's hesitation, she pressed the tiny lever at the back of the drawer to reveal the third and smallest secret compartment. Within lay a silver ring. Hippolyta remembered Catherine's own words to her:

"It is my marriage ring; he was forced to sell his horse to pay for it. In this house, none but you and I know of its existence."

She slipped the ring surreptitiously into one of the pockets under her gown, then began to swab the latticed windows behind the dresser. The aunt looked in to see how she was progressing.

"That is much better," she said.

CHAPTER 4

George woke early the next morning. It was the first time for years that he found himself in such luxurious surroundings. He really had fallen on his feet. As he lay in bed, covered by a white, down-filled duvet, he thought leisurely of his future life at Carshalton Hall. He certainly had no intention of going home now, just when he had been made so welcome and so comfortable. In a moment or two, he would get up. He was looking forward to serving himself scrambled eggs and bacon from silver dishes on the sideboard, and pouring freshly brewed tea from a gleaming silver teapot. He wondered what time it was.

A quarter of an hour later he was walking down the wide staircase leading to the central hallway area. But when he entered the dining room, there was no one there. Obviously it was very early, and the French clock on the mantelpiece confirmed that it was only ten to seven. He thought he heard a noise from behind the swing door and walked through into a servants' corridor leading to the kitchen. The maid from yesterday was there, mopping the kitchen floor. George stood on the threshold, leaning against the doorpost.

"Do you live here?" he asked.

The maid started. "Oh, it's you, sir." George felt uncomfortable at being called sir, especially by someone of his own class. "You're up early."

"So are you." There was a pause.

"Yes, I do live here. None of the other staff do, though."

Ralph walked over to the wooden kitchen table and sat down.

"Does Ralph employ you, or his mother?"

"His mother. But Ralph owns the Hall."

"Really? Would he ever sell it, do you think?"

"Well, not now he couldn't. He doesn't have absolute legal control over it until he's twenty-one. That's when he comes into all the money as well." The maid did not seem to be concerned about volunteering financial information regarding her employers. "And Lady Pulleine comes from a far wealthier family, originally. She has her own money. More than enough to pay for five servants."

"Not servants. Employees, surely."

"I don't know the difference. Excuse me, sir." The maid was mopping underneath the table, now.

"I was under the impression that you were a housemaid."

"This isn't the class of house that employs a separate person for every little thing. I do a bit of everything."

"Do you make cups of tea?"

"You're welcome to make yourself one, sir."

George was happy to oblige. "I'll make you one," he said.

A little later they were both sitting at the kitchen table, the maid opposite George. He learnt that she came from a long line of maids, most of whom had worked at

Carshalton. Various unverifiable stories had been passed down through the generations; stories of extra-marital affairs, bankruptcy, hush-money and other domestic scandals. She told him that her name was Rose and that yes, it was very likely that one of her ancestors would have worked at Carshalton Hall in the early eighteenth century. Perhaps, suggested George, that in the midst of all the scandals, she herself could be related to the Pulleines. Rose thought that this was perfectly possible. A whole hour of animated conversation passed between them, until Rose was suddenly reminded by her conscience of her domestic duties, and jumped up. "Lady Pulleine will be down for breakfast in ten minutes," she said, hurriedly. "I better get on."

Not wishing to encounter Lady Pulleine for a second time, George wandered through the hallway towards the West Wing. He wasn't going anywhere near the dining room until he was sure that the mother had installed herself somewhere for the day and was out of harm's way. He wished she wasn't living there. It would be far more convenient if she just wasn't there.

There appeared to be no sign of Ralph throughout the house. He must still be in bed, thought George, as he approached the large oak door dividing the two parts of Carshalton Hall. It had been left open from the day before. George walked through and a weird feeling of stepping back in time enveloped him. The place had certainly not been given the love and attention it deserved. He crossed through the Blue Drawing-room and into the West Wing hallway. Ascending the dark staircase, he passed the cherub in the recess and reached the landing watched over by the melancholy portraits. Then he rambled casually through the spacious, one-time sumptuous rooms of the first floor of the West Wing. As he did so, the occasional ornament or trinket left upon the dusty mantelpieces caught his inquisitive eye. When he came to the music room, he noticed the clavichord again and wondered if it still worked. He went over to it and lifted the lid, the inside of which was elaborately painted. Trying the keys, he found that only a few of them would sound.

He finally reached the Old Library, situated at the far end of the West Wing. George had begun his search the previous day at the north wall, working his way along the dark, mahogany bookshelves towards the south. In the morning light, he continued his systematic search. The books on the bottom shelf were old and heavy; many of them recorded uninteresting figures concerning the local mining activities. He worked his way along the shelves and up the shelves, until finally, using a three-stepped wooden ladder generously provided by the occupants of centuries gone by, he began to take down books from the top shelf for close examination. It was here, about half-way along, that he found a charming, three volume set, each book the size of a video cover. They were each bound in a light brown leather; gold lettering upon a red band on each of their spines displayed the words, 'SHAFTESBURY'S CHARACTERISTICKS' and the numbers 2, 1 and 3 respectively. Sitting down on the step ladder he carefully opened the second volume past the fly leaf to reveal its title page:

CHARACTERISTICKS &c, Volume II, containing
An Inquiry concerning Virtue and Merit. The
Moralists: a Philosophical Rhapsody.

Below these words was a picture of a firebasket filled with burning wood and below this, the words, Printed in the Year 1711. But George hardly noticed any of this; for in the top right hand corner of the page scrawled in a greyish-purple faded ink was the faded but clear signature of Catherine Pulleine, written in angular, copper-plate handwriting. He turned the pages meticulously; though aged and dust-ridden, the volume gave the appearance of never having been read. The opening chapter appeared to be analysing morals, a subject upon which George was fairly open minded. He attempted to read:

> We know that every creature has a private good and interest of his own, which nature has compelled him to seek by all the advantages afforded him within the compass of his make. We know that there is in reality a right and a wrong state of every creature, and that his right one is by nature forwarded and by himself affectionately sought. There being therefore in every creature a certain interest or good, there must also be a certain end to which everything in his constitution must naturally refer.

If this was all Catherine had had to read and no television, he felt sorry for her; although there was the riding, of course, and the clavichord. And the prospect of marrying some loser. George closed the book and was about to lay it aside with the others when he noticed that there appeared to be something inserted at the back of the third volume, a letter perhaps? But it wasn't a letter, it was the brittle and faded remains of a small flower, pressed hundreds of years ago. An almost imperceptible tinge of blue pervaded its five small petals. George wondered what sort of flower it was. Anxious not to expose it to the elements, he closed the volume again. He would show the set of books to Ralph and Ralph would probably give it to him. For that matter, at what time did Ralph rise, of a morning? In George's experience, the average idler got up at noon. George himself was unusual. He could never sleep past eight. George put the book down carefully on top of the other two. Perhaps he should search the house for 'caches'. A place like this should be riddled with them. Maybe Catherine Pulleine had placed something of importance in one of them and left it there. Or perhaps there might be a dresser somewhere, with a secret compartment. But now he was romanticizing.

The mother had surely finished her breakfast by now. George walked out of the library, carrying the book. As he crossed through into the East Wing and passed through the hallway, through a door ajar he caught sight of the mother, seated in the morning room. George hurried along past the door and into the dining room. He was pleased to see that the table was now laid again, for two. No doubt Ralph would appear in due course. There were, however, no dishes on the sideboard. George sat down at one of the places and waited. Presently the swing door opened and Rose appeared.

"Oh, hello, again. Would you like tea or coffee?"

"Coffee, please."

"Toast and scrambled eggs?"

"Yes, that would be very nice."

Rose disappeared through the door. She did not now seem as conversational as before. When Ralph finally appeared, he was in his dressing-gown. Completely un-abashed by his attire, he beamed at George, hurried up to the table and sat down next to him. George tried to return the warmth but was unable to do so. But he felt that he needed to make an effort.

"Did you sleep well, Ralph?" he said.

Ralph looked slightly embarrassed. "Better than usual. I don't normally get up before twelve. But today, for some reason, I woke up extra early." Then he noticed the lightly speckled, leather-bound book lying on the neighbouring chair.

"Oh, what's that, George?"

George picked up the book and placed it on the table.

"I went back to the library," he said, in a definite tone. "And I found this."

George carefully opened the ageing book near the back. The remains of the tiny flower lay upon the anti-quated printed text of the dried up page. Ralph squinted at it.

"And the book is signed Catherine Pulleine," added George.

"How amazing," said Ralph. "This house must be full of unusual things."

"Yes," said George. The maid reappeared. When she was gone again,

he turned to Ralph.

"Have you any idea what sort of flower this is?" asked George.

"Not exactly," said Ralph. "Though it doesn't look entirely unfamiliar."

"We could look it up on your computer, Ralph."

"I don't have a computer."

George closed the book again. "No, I suppose you wouldn't have."

"There are some books upstairs about wild flowers, though."

"Yes, well, that could be useful."

"I'll go and get them," said Ralph, and bounded out of the room. A moment later, George stood up and walked over to the partition. The door within it was unlocked. He opened it cautiously and looked furtively into the adjoining room, which appeared to be some kind of living room. The furniture and ornaments were mainly of an antique variety; a small wind-up gramophone stood on a low table by the television. Upon the wall was another type of antique clock, set ten minutes slower than the one in the dining room. The Pulleines had certainly spared no expense at one time, long ago. The current occupants were, however, in George's opinion, rather parsimonious. Even the new part of the Hall was starting to look a bit sad. George heard clumsy footsteps coming downstairs. He quickly closed the door in the partition behind him, just before Ralph re-entered the room.

"Here you are," he said, walking straight up to George and holding out a little book. "It's rather old, published in 1936, but it has pictures of all the wild flowers in Northern England. Some of them are in colour."

"Well done, Ralph."

"Let's see the specimen again," said Ralph excitedly, going over to the dining table, and sitting down again. He looked towards George. "Come and sit down again, George," he requested. George obliged. He wondered just what Ralph's feelings towards him were. It was very off-putting and disconcerting to think that he was affecting a member of the same sex in this way, but this appeared to be a necessary evil. He watched as Ralph avidly turned the pages of the floral encyclopaedia, longing to please George with an important finding. His assiduity was soon rewarded, for near the end of the book was a coloured drawing of a tiny plant with five bright blue petals and a short stem.

"It's a spring gentian," said Ralph. "I didn't recognise it at first, what with the petals being so faded."

"I think you're right, Ralph," approved George, glancing over at the vibrant picture in the book. "I really do think you're right."

Ralph beamed with pleasure. "I think it says something down here about the plant," he went on and began to read aloud, in an interested, scholarly voice.

'SPRING GENTIAN

The Spring Gentian (Gentiana Verna) is a tiny plant of height only a few centimetres, distinguished by its striking blue petals, usually 1-2 cm in diameter. Flowering between late spring and early summer, it attracts butterflies and bees (especially bumblebees) for pollination.

The Spring Gentian prefers a dry calciferous soil. It grows in alpine meadows throughout central Europe and also in Upper Teesdale, England and West Burren, Ireland.

According to folklore, if the Spring Gentian is picked, death will soon follow. Should the flower be brought into the house, the individual concerned will risk being struck by lightning.'

Ralph paused, to take in all of this.

"Well, the flower was certainly both picked and brought into the house," he said, finally. "Do you believe in folklore, George?"

"No. Do you?"

"I'm not sure. They go back a long way, superstitions."

"Do you realize how these superstitions were formed, Ralph? One day, someone had a fatal accident and then some woman remembered that the day before the person had picked a spring gentian. So she assumed that the accident had something to do with that. That's how it would have started."

"You're cynical, George."

"Too right I am."

There was another pause.

"Let's see the book," said George. Ralph handed it to him. George was wondering where Catherine Pulleine had picked the spring gentian if indeed she had picked it.

"Where is Upper Teesdale?" he asked.

"About thirty miles North West of here, in County Durham. But I don't think that the specimen came from there."

"The book suggests that it did," argued George.

"The Spring Gentian doesn't only grow in Upper Teesdale," said Ralph. "It can also be found in North Yorkshire in one or two locations. There's a place about seven miles west from here, towards Arkengarthdale, where I have seen it growing."

"Are you sure?"

"Yes. I once saw it growing there, in small clumps, on one of my many walks.

"And you think that's where the specimen came from."

"Oh, not necessarily. But it's a pretty rare plant. There wouldn't be too many places where it could grow."

"Are you sure it wasn't just a similar looking flower that you saw?"

"Well, I suppose it could have been," considered Ralph. "But I'd be surprised. The Spring Gentian has a very distinctive appearance."

George sat back in his seat.

"It's late spring now," he observed.

"Yes," agreed Ralph eagerly. "It's probably growing there now. We could go out there together and have a look if you like."

George decided to push his luck.

"Oh, I really think I should be going," he said. "I've already imposed on you for too long. You've been so very hospitable."

"Don't be ridiculous George. You'll have trouble finding the place on your own. It's actually a ruin of some sort. There's not much left of it. It's not marked on the map; it's just a heap of grass-covered rocks. But I know exactly where it is. We could be there and back by tea-time."

"Well, that's very kind of you, Ralph. In that case, I'd love to go out there with you."

An enraptured smile crossed Ralph's features. "I hope you don't mind walking, George," he said. "There aren't any buses to speak of round there."

"Not at all, Ralph," said George, pleasantly.

Half-an-hour later, Ralph and George were standing in the hallway, preparing to leave. George was wearing an old cagoule that Ralph had loaned him, as it was sure to rain at some point and Rose brought out a lunch bag for them. The mother appeared to have heard the commotion, for she opened the door of the morning room, to disapprovingly observe them walking out of the front door together. George shuddered.

The sky was beginning to cloud over, but it was not raining. It was about half an hour since they had left the house, taking the footpath to Eppleby which ran between the burbling beck shadowed by trees and a vast expanse of yellow maize. Eppleby was about as uninteresting as Aldbrough, if not more so, thought George. Beyond here, the dales opened up before them. They were walking along a narrow verge, alongside a stone wall. Ralph was about three yards ahead.

"We'd better cross the road here," said Ralph. "I can't see the oncoming traffic."

George was starting to get rather fed up with the long walk. "How many more miles, Ralph?" he asked.

Ralph stopped walking and turned around.

"Oh, about another five, George. Don't worry, I know where I'm walking. I know this area like the back of my hand."

"I'm sure you do, Ralph." George continued to trudge along the road. Walking was a pain, he decided. Then he could hear a car coming, so stepped aside. As Ralph did so, he pointed up to some trees in the middle-distance, which appeared to be populated by birds' nests.

"That's a rookery," he said. George looked up at the tree. He thought he had seen trees like that before but had never thought about it. George could not be bothered with rookeries. He mentally added nature to Ralph's list of interests. It was useful to know what made people tick. Up ahead towards the horizon, the sky was black. It was definitely going to rain.

A few miles later, George thought he could see the ruin up ahead. It didn't look like much. It appeared to be just a mound of rocks. As they got closer, however, it seemed to have some kind of structure to it, rising high at one point. Walking towards it they were observed with interest by some neighbouring cows.

"This is it," said Ralph. He sighed and sat down on the nearest rock. The whole ruin was covered thinly with grass.

"That was quite a walk," said Ralph.

George sat down on another rock nearby. A cool, strong breeze was blowing past them. George was vaguely aware of having walked very gradually uphill.

"It sure was, Ralph," he said. He was dreading the walk back.

Ralph got out the sandwiches and began to talk about wildlife again. George was not really listening. He quickly recovered from the physical exertion and stood up again. Remembering why they had come there, he got up and began to wander around, searching systematically for a plant resembling the spring gentian. However, it was nowhere to be seen.

"What are you doing, George?" called out Ralph.

"Spring Gentian," shouted back George, curtly.

"There's one over here, George."

George hurried back to where Ralph was sitting. "Where, Ralph?"

"There." Ralph pointed to a rock slightly higher up. A lone, small flower with petroleum blue petals leant out from the short grass on the rock. It certainly looked like the Spring Gentian.

"My God," said George. He was quite struck by it.

"I wouldn't pick it, though," said Ralph. "It is a rare species."

"I wouldn't dream of it," said George. "Perhaps there are more of them." He began to walk away around the grass covered rocks and soon found a couple more. He began to envisage Catherine Pulleine, on horseback, or on foot, wandering about the ruin. Why had she come here? Had she been alone or accompanied?

George came to the part of the ruin which rose upwards and discovered a roughly arch-shaped hole within one wall. He bent down and stepped through, into a small, grassy rectangular area, measuring about six feet by four feet. It was open up above. The walls were old and grey. George wondered how old. Someone had carved their name and dated it in roman numerals, which came to 1954 by George's reckoning. As he looked around himself, he realized that several other people throughout the ages had left evidence of their visit. A few symbols, insignias and dates were haphazardly scraped into the rock. After a little while, he noticed that low down, near the ground were what were conceivably some letters and numbers. He thought he could make out the letters G A, a space, then C P. Beneath the letters G and A were the numbers 1 and 7; beneath the letters C and P were the numbers 1 and 1. 1711, obviously. The markings were surprisingly clear, as though they had been done yesterday.

"Where are you, George?" Ralph's high voice called out from behind the wall.

"In here, Ralph," answered George, in a resigned tone. He could have done without Ralph right now.

Ralph suddenly appeared and crept in through the hole. "Oh yes, I remember this, now," he said.

"It's a bit cramped in here, Ralph," said George.

"Yes," agreed Ralph, enthusiastically. To George's dismay, he sat down and leant against the wall, partially obscuring the highly significant markings and crossing his feet.

"It's very secluded here," said Ralph.

"Yes," said George, disapprovingly. Finally he sat down, at the wall facing Ralph.

Ralph was staring back at him. There was an uneasy silence. They were sheltered from the breeze in there.

"You say you were here three years ago, Ralph," said George.

"Yes." Or it might have been four. I've been to just about everywhere within a ten-mile radius of Carshalton." Ralph continued to gaze at George, who appeared to be examining the walls. "Yes, there's graffiti all over the inside of the tower. Perhaps we should do some, George."

George got up again and turned back towards Ralph.

"Yes, perhaps we should."

"How about, Ralph and George were here."

"Yes. Or you could write it in Latin, even."

George assumed that Ralph would be fluent in Latin. He stepped out through the archway again, looking all

53

around the grassy, stony plateau and the rolling hills in the near distance. Ralph followed him.

"I've got nothing to carve with, George."

"Oh, there are plenty of rocks lying around."

George sat down on a rock and contemplated. If what he had just seen was not evidence enough of his lineage, nothing was. He looked around for Ralph, who appeared to have disappeared. Presumably, he had gone back into the tower area again. George wandered over to the rock with the brilliant blue gentian, to admire it. It certainly was an exotic flower. George resented being told both by Ralph and the guide book not to pick it. It was none of their business whether he picked it or not. He tugged at it, and it came up easily enough. Then he slipped it into the front pocket of his loaned cagoule. When he got back to Carshalton, he would press it immediately in one of those thick heavy books in the Old Library. Perhaps he would even have it laminated. Then it might last thousands of years, let alone hundreds. Perhaps flower pressing wasn't such a weird hobby after all.

He walked round the ruin and noticed that the clouds were moving in now. There was, fortunately, nowhere to shelter in the rain. Ralph would have loved that. Finally he reached the broken archway again and stepped through. Ralph was inside, carving.

"Ralph, I think we'd better be going. It's going to rain, probably quite heavily."

"Just a minute," murmured Ralph. George glanced at the newly formed scratch marks. It was quite a work of art that Ralph was creating.

When they were finally back on the road, it was already

starting to drizzle. It was going to be awful, walking all the way back in the pouring rain.

"Are you sure there are no bus services around here, Ralph?" asked George, dejectedly.

"Not going past Carshalton. There is a bus from Eppleby to Aldbrough, but we might just as well walk from Eppleby as from Aldbrough. In any case, it's only another four miles. We'll be back before six."

"I suppose so, Ralph." George withdrew into his own thoughts again.

Wandering endlessly along the road, a different attitude began to infiltrate George's mind. Lost in his thoughts, he was forgetting to entertain Ralph, who was walking alongside him, apparently disinclined to try to engage him in conversation for fear of rejection. The Pulleines had lived in luxury for over four hundred years; the Aldersons, however, had had to rough it. It was time that the tables were turned, and he had been sent by Providence to turn them. It was just a question of how.

"Do you have a will, Ralph?" asked George, finally.

Ralph turned to him, glad that he was talking again.

"Well, yes, as a matter of fact, I do. I wouldn't have, only mother ordered me to have one, as I own the Hall. She doesn't want the crown to get their hands on it."

"Wouldn't it go to close relatives?"

"Yes, it would if I had any."

"Well, if you haven't any close relatives, who have you left the Hall to?"

"A cousin on my mother's side. I've only met her twice."

George lapsed into silence again. He still felt very far

away from Carshalton Hall. Another thought struck him.

"When will the will come into effect, Ralph?" he asked.

"On my twenty-first birthday. That's when I come into everything."

"And when is your birthday, Ralph?"

"August the twenty-second."

George made a mental note of this date. It was only about three months away. He quickened his pace and walked ahead of Ralph, but Ralph soon caught up. Ralph was talking to him all the way back, but George was not really listening. He still did not have a plan.

When they arrived back at Carshalton Hall, Lady Pulleine was there in the hallway, lying in wait. She appeared to want to talk to Ralph. Without even apologising to George, she took him into the morning room and closed the door. George had the suspicion that the following conversation, of which he could only catch a few words, concerned him. Then, in the midst of raised voices, it became apparent that Lady Pulleine did not trust Ralph's new friend. The door opened, and Ralph backed out, telling his mother to sack Rose, on the grounds that she was untrustworthy. George was pleased to note that Ralph seemed to have faith in him.

"What was all that about, Ralph?" asked George.

"Oh, mother wants you to leave. She thinks you're going to walk off with the family silver. But it's my house. I want you to stay, George. At least, for a little longer, if you're not busy."

"I am never busy," said George, and smiled broadly at Ralph.

Hippolyta was leaning against the green bark of a young tree in the middle of the orchard at Carshalton, some distance from the house. Beside her lay a wide basket of ripe pears. She took a bite from the largest one, and the sweet juice dripped down her soft face. Her mind was vacuous and open. Her mistress Catherine she had already forgotten.

In the rays of sunlight glinting through the leaves, she thought she could see a man approaching. Was it the master? Why would he come to the orchard? As the man became increasingly visible, she realised that it was the master's son, Wingate. He must have known that she was there. She immediately sat up and smoothed back her thick, mellow hair. In a moment, Wingate appeared in front of her.

After dinner that evening, Ralph sat down at the grand piano in one of the large, sumptuous upstairs rooms of the East Wing. He began to play, singing in a high alto voice.

> "Whilst strolling through the park one day
> All in the merry month of May
> I was taken by surprise by a pair of roguish eyes
> In a moment my poor heart was stole away."

Ralph stopped playing.

"I really like this song," he said. "It has a strange, remote atmosphere about it."

George laughed. "Well, let's hear the rest of it then, Ralph."

Ralph turned back to the piano again.

"I immediately raised my hat
And finally she remarked,
I never shall forget that lovely afternoon
I met her by the fountain in the park."

"It has cycles of fifths in it," said Ralph.

"How exciting," said George.

Ralph turned to George again.

"What would you like to do now, George?" he asked, thoughtfully.

George would have liked to go out somewhere. But there did not appear to be any place to go.

"Are there any pubs around here, apart from The Stanwick Arms?" he asked.

"No," said Ralph. "Do you drink a lot, George?"

"Not to excess." It really was quite a poser, what to do in the evenings at Carshalton.

"Have you got any cards?" he asked, finally.

"I should do," said Ralph, getting to his feet. He walked over to an ivory games table with a chessboard painted onto the top. Opening the lid, he produced a pack of extra large playing cards of an antique, minimalist design.

"They're a bit outsize," he said, examining them. "They're rather old, as well."

George got up from one of the elegant chairs upholstered in silk stripes and walked over to him. "Well, I'm sure they'll do," he said. "As long as they're all there. We'll also need some chips. Do you have any matchsticks?"

"No, but we could use the draughts from the draught set."

There were two chairs, one at each end of the games table. George took the nearest one. "Come on, Ralph, let's get started," he said. Ralph looked awkward and surprised but sat down at once opposite George.

"Oh, I'm not very good at cards, George," he said, apologetically.

"I'll teach you," said George, shuffling the cards in a deft, professional manner, despite their exaggerated size. "We'll start you off with poker. Bring the draughts over."

"Just a minute, George. I'll just turn up the lights. It's a bit dim in here."

Ralph went over to the door. Turning up the dimmer switch he watched as the chandelier bulbs gradually increased to their maximum brightness. The room became less shadowy and gloomy. George waited for him to sit down again, then dealt out the cards. Ralph watched expectantly.

"We are each dealt two cards," he began.

Ralph frowned. "I thought we each got five cards. That's how I vaguely remember it from school."

"That's draw poker. We're playing Texas hold'em poker."

"Oh. That sounds a bit scary, George."

"It's a lot less scary. It's the easiest type of poker."

"OK. If you say so, George."

"You can look at your cards now, Ralph. Actually, you better let me see them."

Ralph laid them carefully out face up on the table.

"You've already got a pair, Ralph. That's a good hand. There would now be a round of betting. I'll explain that in a minute. Now I'm going to deal out three community cards."

Ralph watched as he did so. He was doing his best to concentrate, but he clearly was not a natural. When George dealt out the fifth community card, he explained to Ralph that it was called the river because it was the river on which the players' hopes often went drifting away. Eventually they moved onto a game. George told Ralph what to do at every stage. "Oh, I see, George," Ralph would say, every time. But George was not sure that he did. At one point, Ralph was feeling confident enough to play for real money. But George advised him against it.

"Next time, maybe. Better let you get used to this first," he said.

"It's a bit pointless without money, George," observed Ralph. But he continued to listen dutifully to his sophisticated companion.

By nightfall, George was starting to feel rather tired. Despite being no office worker, he had never really been an evening person. It was hard work, entertaining Ralph. He decided to go to bed.

"I think I'll turn in now, Ralph," he said. "It's getting late."

"Oh. Yes, I suppose it is. Though it's not really late for me."

George stood up. "See you tomorrow, Ralph," he said. "Goodnight."

"Goodnight, George," said Ralph, watching him stride out of the palatial room.

CHAPTER 5

At seven o'clock the next morning George awoke for the second time to the sound of birdsong and the luxury of his new bedchamber. It was Saturday morning. He enjoyed a leisurely breakfast in the dining room overlooking the back of the house and waited for Ralph to come down. The man finally appeared at about nine o'clock, fully dressed and looking more radiant than usual.

"I had such a good night's sleep last night, George," he began, sitting down at the table and pouring out coffee. "I actually slept solidly all night. And when I woke up, I lay awake for about an hour, thinking. And I had a sudden thought."

"Really, Ralph?"

"About why the song I was playing to you yesterday has such a strange, dreamlike quality. The woman is a con artist!"

"Are you sure, Ralph?"

"Yes! She is lying in wait for unsuspecting men at the fountain and then tries to con them."

"Oh, I don't think so, Ralph. She might genuinely like the man in the song."

"I doubt it. "

"You're paranoid, Ralph.

"I'm not. I'm just always in a state of heightened awareness. I'm sure that there's more to the song than meets the eye. You know when something's wrong."

"I'm sure there's nothing sinister intended, Ralph. You've got too much imagination."

"Yes," agreed Ralph. "That's why mother doesn't think much of me."

George could hear Gertrude vacuuming outside the door. Later Rose came in and collected the breakfast things. George glanced at the newspaper that lay on one end of the table. He had forgotten the outside world. But he did not pick it up to read, for fear of ignoring Ralph.

"What would you like to do today, Ralph?" he asked, cheerfully.

"Oh, I'm quite happy doing anything as long as you're here, George."

"Well, what would you normally do?"

Ralph considered this.

"Well, I might go for a walk."

George sighed inwardly. He had been afraid of that. But Ralph had to be kept buttered up at all costs.

"What a lovely idea, Ralph."

Ralph smiled happily. "We could walk to Gilling West, then come back via Richmond."

"Anything you say, Ralph."

George hoped that he could get used to the walking. He had heard that fitness developed quickly on exercising.

An hour later, they were tramping over a field.

"Ralph, this walking's quite exhausting," said George.

"The sooner you find some kind of motorised transport, the better. If we're going to carry on going out like this, we'll need to hire a car."

"I can't drive," said Ralph.

"Oh, yes, so you said. Well, I could drive it."

"You have a driver's licence?"

"Yes. We could get around much more easily than this, Ralph."

"Well, I wouldn't mind travelling by horse and carriage, like they did in the old days," said Ralph. "In the late eighteenth century, if two gentlemen were travelling together, and wanted to explore an area, they'd hire a gig."

"What's a gig?" asked George.

"A type of horse-drawn vehicle with two high wheels," said Ralph. "There's a painting of one in the old part of the Hall."

"With two gentlemen seated on it?"

"Yes."

"Well, I don't think that would have been a good idea round here," said George. "It would have got stuck in the mud."

"Yes, I suppose you're right."

The air was warming up now, and a slight wind was pushing past them.

"You know, you shouldn't put up with your mother's attitude towards you," began George. "I wouldn't stand for it."

"Yes. I suppose it's because I keep expecting her to be nice, and then she comes out with some awful comment."

George was not sure how to respond to this. Then Ralph's voice broke the silence.

"Where are your parents, George?" he asked.

George's parents had dissociated themselves from him.

"They're in London," he replied. From his tone, Ralph appeared to realize that he did not wish to discuss them any further.

As they walked into Richmond, Ralph had some good news for George. There were buses travelling directly from Richmond to Aldbrough. So instead of a seven mile trek home, it would just be a mile across the fields from Aldbrough to Carshalton.

There were no bus stops, but all the buses stopped by the monument. When the right bus finally showed, the driver got off and headed for the shops. George judged that this would be good moment to board the bus. He leapt on and walked straight to the back seats by the window. After a moment's hesitation, Ralph followed him and sat down next to him.

"Aren't we supposed to buy a ticket?" asked Ralph, in a low voice.

"You can," replied George contemptuously. "I'm not."

"What if a ticket inspector gets on?"

"When was the last time a ticket inspector got on?"

"I can't remember."

"Exactly," said George. "You worry too much, Ralph. Relax. Chill out."

Ralph stared nervously out of the window, watching the driver returning to the bus, carrying something. Finally, he said decisively, "Well, I'm going to buy a ticket, even if you're not." He got up and went to the front of the bus. It was a long time since George had bought a ticket, and he wasn't going to start now. He watched as Ralph purchased his precious ticket. Then another member of the bus driving force boarded the bus and began to exchange pleasantries with the driver. Ralph sat down beside George again. They would be sitting there for a good ten minutes, no doubt. George began to feel impatient and irritated. Why on earth couldn't Ralph use a normal form of transport? He glanced around at the outside scene, observing office workers and shop assistants milling about in the town. What boring, drab lives most people lead, he thought. There was so much more to life than the one most people led. He looked back along the bus aisle again and started to see the second driver suddenly walking up towards the back row of seats.

"Can I see your tickets, please?" the man asked politely.

Ralph rummaged hastily in his pocket and produced the necessary bit of paper. The man turned to George. There was a pause. "Where's your ticket?" he asked, in a slightly concerned tone.

"I haven't bought it yet," said George, lamely.

"Well, your friend has bought his," said the man.

"I didn't realize that the bus was about to leave," said George.

"You need a ticket just to sit on the bus," said the driver, shortly.

"I didn't know that," said George.

"Would you like to step off the bus now, sir."

George sighed and got up. But as he walked along the bus aisle he reminded himself that paying fines was cheaper than buying tickets. As he stood with the driver outside the bus, he offered to pay the penalty fare, but in a business like tone, the driver insisted on seeing identification. George began to feel slightly worried. Surely he did not look guilty and criminal enough for the Magistrates Court? He was vaguely aware that Ralph was now standing beside him. George produced his driver's licence. The driver come inspector took this from him and wrote down the details slowly and carefully. Then without any more ado, he handed it back to George without looking at him and walked away. George glanced at Ralph. It did not seem appropriate to get back onto the bus. A moment later, its engine started up. Then it drove off.

"I'm so sorry about this, George," said Ralph, sympathetically. "That really was rotten luck."

"Oh, it doesn't matter," said George.

"You're not looking for work, so it doesn't matter if you get a criminal record," said Ralph.

George felt reassured by this. "Thank you, Ralph," he said, smiling wanly at him.

In the music room, Hippolyta swept the dust rag lightly over the open painted lid of the clavichord. The mistress of the house was tolerant of her condition, and she no longer did any heavy work. Wingate Pulleine had not been seen at Carshalton for over six months and was possibly unaware of her situation. For a moment she stopped dusting and with one hand, unevenly played out a familiar tune upon the keys. In the effort and concentration of hitting the right notes, she did not immediately hear the approaching footsteps and voices but seconds later identified them to be that of Thomas Pulleine, unexpectedly visiting, and the aunt. The master had not on any account to see her. She broke off playing and leaving the rag carelessly behind upon the clavichord stool she hastened through the doorway towards the Gallery. There she lifted the heavy tapestry that hung upon one wall and disappeared behind it.

It was about five-thirty when they finally arrived back at the Hall. They had remained in a reasonably dry state until the last minute when the heavens had opened. They got into the hallway of the house after the final dash across the front lawn. George removed his dripping wet cagoule and Ralph took it from him, then handed it to Rose, who had suddenly appeared from nowhere. But his trousers were soaked through. He went upstairs to the guest room to freshen up before dinner. There was no way that Ralph would be kicking him out now. On the newly-made bed lay a pair of dark blue corduroy trousers and an ironed chequered shirt, which were only marginally too large for him. Ralph must have given Rose instructions to clothe him, for the mother would never have organised such a thing.

Half an hour later he was back downstairs again. Ralph was at the bottom of the stairway. He had also changed clothes. "Ah, there you are, George," he said. "I'm afraid it's another hour or two until dinner. Rose and the cook have got behind again."

"Well, what shall we do in the meantime, Ralph?" asked George, in as friendly a tone as he could muster.

"Um …. Well, it's raining outside, so we have to stay indoors. I've already shown you most of the house. I suppose you're probably sick of the house, anyway."

"Oh, no, not at all, Ralph."

"Oh. Well, in that case, I could show you the old servants' quarters on the second floor of the West Wing."

A flicker of interest sparked in George's mind.

"Yes, why not, Ralph," he said.

They went through the old oak door, into the musty atmosphere of the West Wing, up the central stairway, past the portraits and the cherub, then up a second staircase, which was covered in a rough brown carpet, to the second floor, which had sloping ceilings and wonky, exposed beams. There was a middle area with ill-fitting doors leading off it. This part of the house was the mustiest of all. At one wall was a dust-covered glass cabinet, containing a doll, dressed in a yellow tutu.

"I don't think I've been up here for years," said Ralph. "In fact, I don't think anybody has."

"That's more than likely, Ralph," said George.

Ralph walked over to the nearest door, which had old, white paint peeling off it. He turned the doorknob which appeared to be loose and looked in. "I think this was a servant's room at one time," he said, stepping out of the way to allow George to walk past him. It was uncomfortably small and empty except for a metal bed with a coarse, moth-eaten mattress upon it. At the end of the room, the rain lashed heavily against a circular window, like a porthole, giving the impression of being on a ship in a storm.

"Well, at least it was probably a single room," said George, walking forwards. "There's nothing worse than room sharing." It was getting dark now, and there was no light switch. Without a word of warning, his foot suddenly went through the floor.

"Oh, careful, George, the floorboards are very aged and fragile," said Ralph. "It's better not to tread too heavily."

George retrieved his leg and picked up the broken piece of narrow, darkened plank. "I think you've got some dry rot here, Ralph," he cautioned.

"Have I? I've never really managed to work out exactly what dry rot is."

Ralph walked out again. "There are several rooms like this one up here," he said as George followed him back into the central area. Ralph tried the handles of two other doors, but they appeared to be locked. "Maybe they're just stuck, Ralph," suggested George, and was about to help. But then Ralph succeeded in opening the door to the room at the end; it turned out to be quite a lot larger than the others. The walls were lined with bookshelves stacked with old books and magazines, and the floor was covered with old trunks and suitcases; when they lifted the lid of one, it was found to contain postcards and letters. Someone years ago had left the window open, and a gentle breeze was blowing the nearby papers about. George stepped over the trunks and stood looking out of the window. A rickety iron ladder ran down the brick wall from just under it to the ground fifty feet below. Ralph came over and tried shutting the window, but it was jammed fast.

"I don't remember leaving the window open," said Ralph. "Though I can't honestly remember for sure if it was closed the last time I was in here, which was some time ago. When I was a child, I think the door to this room was usually locked."

"Well, it seems like it was used as a storage room at one time, and no one ever bothered to clear it out," said George.

"Well, I'm certainly not going to," said Ralph.

There was a pause.

"What now, Ralph?" asked George.

"Well, that's it, as far as the house is concerned," replied Ralph. "If it wasn't pelting down I could have shown you around the grounds. Perhaps we should just go downstairs again for an aperitif in the drawing-room."

"Good idea, Ralph."

They went out again and over to the staircase. But as George took a first step, he felt his foot slip forwards on the stair carpet, and in an instant, he had lost his balance and fell headlong down the stairwell. Fortunately he was quick to react, and his hands took the impact. On reaching the bottom, his wrist was very sore and painful.

"My God, George, are you all right?" called out Ralph, from the top of the stairs.

George glanced up at him and noticed that the stair rod on the second step from the top was missing, causing the carpet to slip forwards.

"I think so," he replied, reassuringly. "Though you really should be more careful about the stair carpets, Ralph. Someone could get killed."

"Oh, I am dreadfully sorry," said Ralph. "It's just that hardly anyone ever enters the West Wing nowadays, so it hardly seems worth fixing everything."

"Yes, well," said George disapprovingly. He was sitting on the bottom step, nursing his wrist. Ralph hurried down the steps and sat down next to George.

"Is your wrist all right?" asked Ralph, tentatively.

George looked at him sardonically.

"I'm really not sure, Ralph," he said. But his wrist was hurting a bit less now.

Ralph reached out to feel George's wrist, to find out if

it was broken, but George stopped him and assured him that it wasn't. He was sure it was just sprained if that. So they went downstairs again, and sat on the large, oak chairs in the ground floor hallway, waiting for dinner. The rain was now ever more intense. Without warning, there was a blinding flash of lightning which lit up the dim hallway and an almost simultaneous crack of thunder, like a muffled gunshot. George thought he felt the house shake. The thunder rolled away into the distance.

"It's quite an exciting storm, isn't it, Ralph," said George.

"I love thunderstorms," said Ralph, smiling happily. "I think it's moving away now, though."

"Did you bag any of these, Ralph?" asked George, indicating the trophy animal heads all around the hallway.

"I've never even held a gun," said Ralph. He pointed to the gun rack by the stairs, stacked with rifles. "My father used to shoot the rabbits on the lawn with those," he said. "That is about my only memory of him."

"Are they still loaded?" asked George.

"No, definitely not. That would be too dangerous," said Ralph.

When the dinner gong finally sounded, and they came into the dining room, George was further disconcerted to see the mother, seated at what should have been his place at the dining room table. He attempted to smile politely at her, but it ended up as a grimace. The rain was still hammering at the French windows. Making a tremendous effort, George spoke to the mother.

"It's quite a storm, isn't it?" he said.

"Summer storms are not at all unusual," was the reply. It's not really summer yet, thought George. They sat down. George's wrist was starting to hurt again, now. Ralph seemed to notice George's expression of pain.

"George has had a little accident, mother," he explained. "Up on the second floor of the West Wing. He fell down the stairs."

"Really. How on earth did he manage that?"

"The stair carpet's loose. George fell on his wrist."

The mother glanced uninterestedly at George's right wrist.

"He could have broken his neck," she observed, in a somewhat unsympathetic tone.

"Yes, mother, you're right." Ralph paused in his speech and took a slight breath. "You know, mother, I've been thinking, perhaps we should take some of my money to do up the West Wing. There are so many things needing doing there."

"Well, neither of us is going to live in the West Wing," replied the mother, abrasively. "And the East Wing is perfectly all right. I was going to allow you some of the money for your university education, but you failed your A-levels."

"Oh, no, not that again, mother."

"I don't like the way you have been behaving lately, Ralph," went on the mother. "You seem to have lost all direction and purpose."

"I never had direction and purpose."

"Well, at least you were active at school."

"How do you know?"

"Well, I assume you were."

"Yes. You just assume things."

There was a pause. They began the soup. George's spoon was solid and heavy, presumably made of sterling silver, and the bowl was of an antique blue and white Chinese design. George had never had freshly-made mushroom soup with sherry added to it, and he began to feel very much at home. He had almost forgotten about his awful flat. He looked about himself curiously every now and again but felt it best not to say anything.

Ralph suddenly broke the silence.

"George will be staying with us for a little while longer," he announced.

The mother did not answer. Then Rose came in through the swing door again and collected up the soup plates, then left. The swing door shut with a woomph behind her. They sat in silence and waited for the next course.

Against his better judgement, George decided to ask the mother a polite question.

"Do you have a university education, Lady Pulleine" he enquired.

For the first time, Lady Pulleine looked George in the eyes. They were grey, disappointed and critical.

"No. I went to a finishing school in Switzerland."

"Of course. How silly of me," George reprimanded himself. With a well-sculptured, manicured hand, he lifted the bottle of Chardonnay from the metal ice-bucket.

"Would you like some more wine, Ralph?" he said.

Ralph looked pleased and delighted.

"Oh, thank you, George." He allowed George to pour, watching as the red liquid glugged into his empty crystal glass.

"Have you made any further developments concerning your genealogical connections?" butted in the mother, suddenly. George looked towards her.

"No," he said. "But I'm fairly confident, all the same."

"You have far too much confidence for my liking," retorted the mother.

"Thank you," said George.

Shortly after the desert, the mother left the table, rather ungraciously, in George's opinion. She shuffled out of the room, hopefully heading for her personal headquarters. When she was finally out in the hallway, he experienced a sudden relief of tension. He had thought she would never leave. Everything seemed to be going moderately well, now.

"How's your wrist, George?" asked Ralph.

"Oh, I think it'll be all right," said George. "I think I just twisted it."

"I hope so. I presume you're not going to sue us," added Ralph, with a nervous laugh.

George smiled wickedly. "Now, there's an idea, Ralph," he said.

Ralph stood up abruptly. "Shall we withdraw to the drawing-room, George?" he asked.

"Why ever not?" replied George.

Ralph threw open the door in the partition to reveal the room at which George had already taken a peek two days earlier. He walked in, and after a moment's hesitation, he wound up the antique gramophone, then took a seventy-eight out of its browned sleeve and placed it upon the turntable. Amidst crackles, a light, tenor voice crooned out an old number that George did not recognise. Soon, they were seated, drinks beside them; Ralph was upright in a red leather armchair, and George was reclining leisurely on a red chaise longue. The only trouble with Carshalton Hall was that there weren't any proper sofas for him to lie on. Very soon, the music stopped.

"Mother was a bit off, this evening," Ralph was saying.

"You can say that again," said George. "I don't know why you let her treat you like that. After all, she is living in your house."

"She has right of occupancy."

"Oh," said George, in a perturbed tone. He had not thought of that. That could be quite a nuisance.

"Will she still have right of occupancy when you turn twenty-one?" he asked.

"Oh, yes. Her right of occupancy is permanent and incontestable."

George glanced out of the windows. It was dark now, and he could just about make out the form of the trees at the edge of the woodland past the beck. He could no longer hear the sound of rain against the panes.

"I shouldn't worry about the Magistrates Court," said Ralph. George had forgotten about the Magistrates Court. "The worst they can do is fine you."

"And give me a criminal record."

Ralph looked ponderous. "Well, you don't really need a clean slate if you're living here," he concluded. This was music to George's ears.

CHAPTER 6

The following afternoon, Ralph announced that he had a dentist's appointment. George would have accompanied him, but had a phobia for dental surgeries, and explained this to Ralph. Ralph completely understood.

"That's quite all right, George. You stay at the Hall until I get back."

"Don't be long," called out George, standing on the doormat, as Ralph walked out through the front entrance and into a waiting taxi that would take him into Darlington.

Rose was hovering; George stepped away as she closed the front door behind Ralph. He walked back into the hallway. Now he was free to roam about the old part of Carshalton Hall admiring the artefacts. He had actually considered disposing of some of them, but had decided against this obvious course of action; for one thing, he was not acquainted with any fences. The only person he could pass anything of any value onto was a Hi-Fi salesman of sorts that he knew; but he was not about to jeopardise Ralph's trust in him.

It was amazing how careless with their property rich people could be. The old wing was falling into decay. George was sure that the wood was riddled with dry rot.

Plaster had fallen off the ceiling in several places, and some of the small, square panes in the latticed windows were broken. As he walked through the Divan Room, George decided that, when he was Lord of the Manor, he would strip the wallpapers back to the bottom layer, which he would then preserve. The room would look just as it had when Catherine Pulleine had lived there. The idea fascinated him; he strolled around, looking in drawers and closets. In one place he found a tray of miniature porcelain tea bowls and teapot. George picked up one of the bowls and turned it over, to discover a blue 'c' marked on the base.

"You'll have trouble getting rid of that." A woman's voice behind him made him start. It was Rose. George put down the tea bowl.

"What makes you think I'm getting rid of it?"

"Madam asked me to check up on you. She thought you might be up to something like this. I thought so myself, in fact."

"Really?"

"All I want to know sir, is, what's in it for me?"

"Nothing's in it for you." George walked past Rose, ignoring her. Then from a distance, he turned to face her.

"And I'm not just talking about the antiques," he added, then strode off, towards the Gallery.

The Gallery had a Tudor look about it; the dark, square panelling gave the room a closeted feel. George wandered over to where the enigmatic portrait of Catherine Pulleine still hung. He now took it for granted that it was her. He studied it carefully, at his leisure. He had almost completely forgotten about Anne. Anne now appeared selfish and soulless, whereas this new woman was thoughtful and spiritual. What was it that he had seen in Anne? He really could not remember.

George recollected once having been obliged to visit an old, rambling manor house, in Somerset or Dorset, haphazardly built. There had been a room there, in the West Wing, with walls lined with oak panelling just like in this Gallery, in which a door was concealed. The door had been placed slightly open; George had peeked in to see a narrow, staircase leading upwards; although it was probably not allowed, when nobody appeared to be looking, George had ascended the staircase up to a locked door. He had come back down again; as he was about to re-emerge, he had heard a guard telling two American tourists not to go up further than a couple of steps, for they were rickety and damaged. Well, it's too late now, he had thought, coming back into the room again. But in any case, might such a thing not also exist here? Perhaps oak panelling was a sign of secret doors. The only wall in the room that could possibly be thick enough for a secret passage was the one covered by the tapestry. George walked over to the heavy canvas, the sound of his heels resounding throughout the room. Watched impassively by the stuffed owl from within the bell-jar, he bent down to lift it, half expecting it to disintegrate in his hands but its thick, rough texture suggested that it was hardier than that. Behind it was the same oak panelling. As he rapped systematically on each of the dark wooden rectangles constituting the panelling, he came across an area where the sound was hollow. George smiled. With a slight push, the section opened inwards with only a slight resistance to reveal a tiny, spiral staircase within the thickness of the wall. The door had possibly not been opened for two or three centuries. George stepped in. He took a couple of paces up the wooden steps, barely deep enough for his feet, stopped momentarily, then took another few steps. They appeared to be holding his weight. The staircase wound tightly round a pillar, up into the semi-darkness. Assuming that the construction was still sound, he stepped carefully upwards to a little landing on the floor above, surrounded by a balustrade; in front of him was a door, identical to the one below. It was not locked, but as he pushed it, he found it to be blockaded by a heavy trunk. But he managed to shove that aside.

George found himself standing in the storeroom with the books and suitcases. The door was actually a vertical section of the bookshelves. Why did Ralph not show me this, yesterday, he wondered. Did the heir to Carshalton Hall even know about it? It did not appear so. Even more so than on the day before, papers were blowing about, as in a gale; then he saw that part of the ceiling had caved in; amidst burnt out beams the cloudy sky now brooded visibly through the slanting roof. It must have happened during the storm. Ralph would be pleased.

Walking out into the central area again, he saw that the door to the little servant's room nearest the stairs had been left ajar from the day before. On an afterthought, George entered. He could see virtually nothing through the circular windowpane, as it was clouded and dirty. He lifted the worn and ragged mattress, then let it fall back upon the iron bed. Copious amounts of dust and dirt emanated from it. Then he crouched down and stared through the broken area and under the narrow, dark, floorboards. There, groping around, he came across what looked like a blackened silver ring and antique sewing scissors lying underneath them; there seemed no harm in pocketing them, so he did. Then he came out of the room again, into the main area.

The floor stretched over the ground space of the house, but in the middle area, it was possible to look all the way down the staircase to the ground floor hallway. The banisters in this place had a coarse, fibrous appearance, and were lighter in colour than the rest of the wood around. George applied a slight pressure to the banister and felt it giving way slightly. He applied more pressure; the banister gave way still more, and George realised that anyone leaning on it would probably fall head first into the hallway two floors below if they lost their balance, which they probably would, under such circumstances. George released the pressure. He did not wish to damage the property of others. Satisfied that it still looked reasonably intact, he walked away from it, towards the stairwell. He was careful not to trip this time. It would be all too easy to have a fatal accident up in the servants' quarters; rickety banisters, unfastened stair carpets, not to mention that old, iron fire escape leading vertiginously down from the storeroom on the outside of the house; perhaps it was not fastened very securely.

George returned to the guest room and placed the rusted silver ring and scissors upon the chest of drawers by the window. He was particularly interested in the ring. Judging from its size and delicateness, it was probably intended for a woman. He felt sure that it was much older than the scissors. If he cleaned it up, it would be as good as new.

George nipped into the en suite bathroom and grabbed the tube of toothpaste that lay untidily with the top off at one end of the sink. Perhaps it would not be the best cleaning solution, but it was to hand. Sitting down on the bed again, he squeezed a little out and dabbed it all over the ring. A silvery lustre magically began to reappear. George held up the ring in delighted admiration; there was an inscription around the outside, just decipherable as 'all I refuse and thee I choose.' How nice. He wondered if there was a hall mark. There would have to be one if it was real, sterling silver. There did appear to be several tiny markings, inscribed within the inner circumference. All I need now is a catalogue of hall marks, he thought, industriously. I am sure there must be one here. That is just the sort of book they would have. It would still be a little while before Ralph got back. The new library he was aware was just a few doors down from the guest room. It would not take a moment to go and have a look. George went there immediately. It was a fairly modern looking room and not particularly large; there was nothing in the room except books. The shelves were ordered in some way, but it was not obvious exactly how. He soon found a volume with a grey cover entitled 'Jackson's silver and gold marks', for his consultation. He had the silver ring with him and was attempting to date its manufacture. There were three markings visible; apparently one was the certificate of authenticity, one was the maker's mark, and one was the date. The date would be in the form of a letter of the alphabet, as on car registration plates. The letter inscribed on the ring resembled a P, but he could not be quite sure. Deep in concentration, he did not notice the figure of Lady

Pulleine crossing the threshold and approaching him.

"What are you doing?" she barked, in an accusing tone. George nearly jumped out of his skin.

"Nothing," he said, immediately closing the book. He felt totally unprepared.

"I would prefer it if you did not freely wander around the house as you do," she said. She was about a foot shorter than him.

"Well, what do you expect me to do?"

"Well, I would prefer it if you were not here at all."

"The feeling is mutual," said George. He replaced the book upon the slightly dusty shelf. The ring had been cut around about seventeen eleven. He would come back later when the mother was not around, to further check the details.

"I will leave if and when Ralph tells me to," he added, walking away. He went straight back to his room. It was at times like this that he appreciated its seclusion. He switched on the television and made himself a cup of coffee. Then he sat on the bed, holding the porcelain cup and saucer, sipping pensively. He began to think about the ring again. 1711. That was the year that was carved upon the ruin, under the initials GA and CP. It was the year before George Alderson alias Pulen was born. From its craftsmanship, it was obviously a gentlewoman's ring. In his head and his heart, he knew it belonged to Catherine Pulleine. It was now in his safekeeping. He could imagine her delicate hands and her wrist. She would not have worn it overtly, he was sure, for her marriage into the lowly Aldersons would undoubtedly have been clandestine. But how had it ended up in the servant' quarters? George's train of thoughts was suddenly interrupted by the sound of an approaching taxi along the gravelled pathway. Ralph was home. He decided not to bother telling Ralph about the secret staircase, or the ring. He walked out of the room and downstairs, to greet Ralph on his return from the dentist.

George stood in the ground floor hallway, waiting for the front door to open. When it did, Ralph walked straight into the house and towards the old part of the manor. "The house was struck by lightning last night," he said, in a purposeful, concerned tone. "The taxi driver pointed it out to me as he drove in. There's a huge gaping hole in the roof of the West Wing." George followed him upstairs, to the servants' quarters and into the storeroom. "My God," Ralph kept saying, over and over again as he gazed up at the ceiling in devastation.

"Doesn't the house have a lightning conductor?" asked George, incredulously.

"Yes. But it's situated on the East Wing."

"Sounds like you were quite unlucky, Ralph."

"Well, yes. You'd have thought we'd be safe, what with all the trees around. Though theoretically, it is advisable to have a series of lightning conductors along the entire length of the manor. It's going to cost a fortune to fix this."

Ralph was sounding surprisingly alert and alive, thought George. Emergencies seemed to agree with him. The young man was looking around, examining the extent of the damage.

"I say, George, do you realise, we could have been up here when the lightning struck."

"Yes," said George. "I do."

A little later, they were downstairs in the kitchen,

drinking tea. The lightning had been a major talking point.

"I'm surprised that the old oak tree at the bottom of the lawn wasn't hit," said George. "That must be the tallest thing around."

"Yes," said Ralph. "I believe it has been hit before now. The inside of it is completely hollow."

"Well, I never," said George.

"What did you do while I was out?" asked Ralph.

"Oh, I just sat in my room for a while," said George.

"Oh. I hope you weren't too bored."

"Oh, no," said George. "You weren't away for very long."

Ralph smiled. George's thoughts began to wander back to the ring. It was nothing less than proof that George Alderson had married Catherine Pulleine. In other words, George Alderson alias Pulen was not an illegitimate Pulleine, as he had previously supposed, but a legitimate Alderson; therefore he himself was not a Pulleine after all, but a common Alderson. But he was still a Pulleine by blood. Why should Ralph be any more entitled to the Pulleine legacy than he was?

"I hope that you are feeling at home, here," said Ralph. "Feel free to treat the place as though it was your own home."

"I will try to, Ralph," replied George, affably.

CHAPTER 7

The next few days were rather tedious. George had been initially inspired by Carshalton Hall, but now Ralph's company was starting to take its toll. However, he continued to try and keep Ralph happy at all times. Sometimes Ralph wanted to play cards, other times he wanted to go out walking. He had even tried to teach George to play the piano, but George found that too arduous. George was managing to keep out of the mother's way, most of the time. He often bumped into Rose, in the corridors and hallways of the Hall, perhaps a little too often. He did not return her smiles.

Then on the Friday of that week, the statuette of the nude cherub in the wall recess below the landing of the West Wing disappeared. Rose had obviously reported the matter to the mother, for both Ralph and George were summoned to the morning room, where Rose and the mother sat, waiting. Rose seemed reluctant to speak, but the mother lost no time in accusing George of theft of personal property. She began by telling George that he was a parasite and now a thief as well, but did not dwell on the loss of the antique; instead, she seemed more concerned with removing George from the house.

"I want you to leave immediately," she concluded.

"Now, hang on, mother," complained Ralph. "How can you possibly be sure it was George?"

"Because the theft only occurred after George arrived," returned the mother immediately. "My servants don't steal. And Hippolita would hardly report a theft if she herself had perpetrated it."

"I don't see why not," said George. He was fairly sure that Rose was responsible.

"It weren't me," said Rose, from the sofa.

There then followed a silence, which Ralph presently broke.

"Are you sure you didn't send it out somewhere yourself, and then forgotten about it?"

"Of course not. I would not forget a thing like that."

"I'm surprised you even know about the statuette, mother," said Ralph. "You haven't been in the old wing for ever such a long time."

"I know about every antique in the house," replied the mother, with irritation. "It was bought by my husband's grandfather on his travels in Italy. I shall be very upset if it is not returned."

"Well, we'll see what can be done," said Ralph.

"That is not good enough," responded the mother, emphatically.

Ralph sighed. "Well, what do you want me to do?"

"I want you to tell George to leave the house."

"I don't want to do that. I know it wasn't George."

The mother was silent. The nearest clock ticked loudly.

"Come on, George," Ralph said finally. "I don't think there's any point in continuing this discussion." George was more relieved than he cared to admit. Every second in the mother's presence was an ordeal. As Ralph and he exited the room, he heard Rose conversing with the mother about exactly when she had noticed that the statuette was gone. She seemed unsure.

"You do realize that I believe you, George," said Ralph, once they were out in the hallway again. "I know you're not a common, petty thief. You've too much class for that."

George smiled. "I'm glad you're such a good judge of character, Ralph," he said.

As they walked upstairs together, George asked, "Why does your mother call Rose 'Hippolita?'"

"Mother calls the servants by whatever names she pleases," he answered. "I believe that Hippolita is Rose's middle name."

George and Ralph had gone back up to the room with the grand piano where they had been playing backgammon on an old set, sitting on the ivory inlaid chairs at the games table. But now, both had lost interest. Ralph was now at the piano, and George was standing by the window with his hands in his pockets, gazing out of the window which faced the front lawn.

"Modal keys went out in the eighteenth century," Ralph was saying. "I'm not sure why the Ionian mode is always used now. There must be something special about it."

"Yes, Ralph," agreed George, trying to maintain his interest. A slightly alarming sight had met his eyes. A car marked 'POLICE' on one side was slowly rounding the gravelled pathway. When it reached the house, two uniformed men got out and walked over to the front door. They had a rather unconcerned look about them, as though they had come only because they had at that moment nothing better to do.

"I think your mother has called the police," George said quietly, continuing to stare out of the window.

Ralph hurried awkwardly over to where George was standing. "I was afraid of that," he said. Then, with surprising decisiveness, he said, "Quick, down the servants' stairs. We can slip out the back door."

"That will look suspicious, Ralph. Anyway, I thought we'd agreed that I didn't take the statuette."

"Yes, but you have that Magistrates Court order coming up. The last thing you want is more mud on your face."

"I'd rather just stay here, Ralph. They may not want to see me, anyhow."

The police did not stay long. Within ten minutes they were walking out of the door again, and getting back into their car, without any more ado. George came away from the window and smiled at Ralph, who was now looking a little sheepish.

"They probably weren't too impressed with your mother's plight," he said.

Hippolyta stood before Thomas Pulleine in the Blue Drawing-room. Her physical condition was obvious. "It were Wingate," she proclaimed.

It was true that Wingate had briefly stayed at the Hall, during his vacation from the University. Thomas Pulleine decided to assume responsibility. From a small money chest, he produced three gold sovereigns and shoved them over the table towards the woebegone maid. He then instructed her to leave Carshalton Hall at once. With a cry of anguish, Hippolyta scrambled out of the room.

Late that evening, George had something to attend to. Soon after Ralph had gone to bed, he headed for Rose's room, which was situated on the first floor of the East Wing, and was actually rather similar to his, with en suite facilities provided. As he approached it, light was streaming from underneath the door, and the sound of someone moving about inside was audible. George knocked purposefully upon the door.

"Who is it?" a female voice called out.

"It's George."

"Just a minute."

George waited. Presently the door opened. Rose was wearing a pink towel around her generous young body and another, identical looking towel as a turban on her head. George walked in without being invited.

"About the statuette," he began.

"I haven't got it," said Rose.

George was slightly concerned that the thefts would continue and that complications concerning his presence at Carshalton would arise. Sitting down on the bed, he explained to Rose the possible consequences of the dangerous game that she was playing. Rose stared at him, half in admiration, half in fear. She removed the towel from her head and allowed her dripping wet, wavy hair to fall about her lovely shoulders. George decided to stay a bit longer.

When he got back to his room, he was feeling rather tired. It was raining persistently, and the air had turned unusually cold for May. He closed the window and hardly undressing, fell into bed and was asleep within seconds.

In the morning, Rose was serving at breakfast. George

could not bring himself to talk to her. He answered her attempt at cheerful questions with as short an answer as possible and did not look at her. Rose finally left the dining room and did not return for the remainder of the meal. George slipped out in the usual furtive manner that he had adopted since moving into Carshalton Hall and began to plan his day with Ralph. Fortunately Ralph was not particularly demanding; merely a bit tiresome.

When Ralph came down at eleven, George sat with him at the breakfast table. George had a question for him.

"Can you swim, Ralph?"

"Yes. I started learning at school, but couldn't cope. So mother paid for me to have private swimming lessons during the vacations. She was worried about me drowning."

"That's not like her."

"Oh, she can be OK, sometimes."

George fell silent again. He had had a feeling that Ralph would be able to swim, despite his somewhat pathetic appearance.

"I can also ride a bike," said Ralph, attempting to keep up the conversation. "Though I'm a bit wobbly. I haven't got a very good sense of balance."

"Why do you think that is?"

"I don't know. I think it has something to do with the middle-ear."

"You don't seem to be a hundred percent fit, Ralph."

"Oh, I am really. My grandfather lived to ninety-five."

George waited patiently and politely as Ralph ate.

"Well, what shall we do today?" he asked when Ralph's breakfast finally appeared to be over.

"You ask me that every morning. It's a question I never used to bother myself with until you came. Perhaps it is important to do things."

"Oh, probably not, Ralph."

"We could do some more genealogical investigation. You never found out for sure if you were descended from my family."

"No, I didn't."

"Well, shall we go back to the library and do some more research? What about the book signed by Catherine Pulleine, with the pressed flower?

"What? Oh, that. Well, it doesn't really help with my genealogy."

"No, but it's interesting, all the same. Where is the book now?"

"It's in my room."

"Oh. Well, you can have it, if you like. I don't know how much it's worth."

"Thank you very much, Ralph."

CHAPTER 8

The days passed. George was now accustomed to getting up at ten-thirty, or eleven. He was even starting to experience the feeling of 'ennui,' that the middle-class and upper-class often spoke about. Perhaps he wasn't getting anywhere. Then he reminded himself that Ralph's trust in him was increasing daily and that Ralph's relationship with his mother was deteriorating rapidly. George did not dare to let Ralph out of his sight, lest he should lose control of the situation. He was tempted to take the bus into Newcastle and visit the casinos, but remained at the Hall, babysitting Ralph. The mother was becoming less and less mobile. Once seated in one seat, she would rarely budge from it for hours. He was playing a waiting game. The question was, how long would he have to wait? Just recently he had taken to frequenting The Stanwick Arms without Ralph. It was on one such evening, when Ralph was at the other end of the Hall, that he slipped out for a pint. Derek was there. Derek was the only customer with whom he was able to have a semi-decent conversation. Though Derek's conversation was, in his opinion, ultimately lacking. Several pints later, he staggered back to the Hall, which was now in darkness, and up to his room. He closed the window and changed into shorts and a T-shirt.

It was about a quarter past eleven. George decided to go downstairs to the kitchen and get a beer. Everything was quiet as he crossed the landing. The stairs creaked slightly as he descended them. On reaching the kitchen, he switched on the light. Everything had been tidied up and put away. He collected a couple of cans from the fridge, switched off the light and went upstairs again. Once back in his room, he turned on the television and fell onto the bed.

A few minutes later there was an uncertain knock at the door. George got up and opened it. Outside stood Ralph, a bottle of wine in one hand and two glasses in the other. He appeared to have changed into better clothes and looked worried and nervous.

"I noticed that you were up, George, so I thought that perhaps we could have a drink together."

George looked at him in a slightly bored fashion.

"Well, I suppose so. Come on in, Ralph."

Ralph sighed, and walked in.

"I've got the best wine imaginable," he said, placing the glasses on the dressing table. He produced a corkscrew from his trouser pocket. "It was bottled in '89. That was one of the best years ever for Chardonnay. I've been saving it for a special occasion." He tried to open the bottle but appeared to be having trouble again, so George assisted. Ralph poured the wine and handed George a glass, staring meaningfully into his eyes. George looked away, somewhat displeased, then sat down on the bed. Ralph immediately sat down, close to him.

"I really am glad you decided to stay, George," he began, moving even closer. "Really, really glad."

George stared into his glass. Nothing ever went smoothly. There was always something that had to be borne.

"I've never met anyone like you before, George," went on Ralph. "You're so masculine."

George decided that he could not go through with this. There were limits to what he was prepared to put up with, in order to gain his rightful place in life. He stood up then went to the door and held it open.

"I'm really very tired, Ralph. Perhaps you could come back some other time."

The expression on Ralph's face changed dramatically. Previously he had been agog and aglow. He now looked sad and annoyed. Then he walked straight out of the room without looking at George.

George closed the door again, and then on an after thought, locked it. He didn't want Ralph returning during the night with some silly excuse. Then he slumped back on the bed again, turning on the television with the remote control. He wondered if he had blown it with his designs on Carshalton Hall.

But the following day, Ralph was all apologies.

"I don't know what came over me last night, George," he said, as they sat at the breakfast table. George had said nothing for several minutes after sitting down, apart from a curt good morning. "I wasn't thinking. I didn't realise you were tired."

George looked at him questioningly.

"Yes, well, it was a bit late, Ralph."

"Anyway, I thought I'd take up your suggestion of

hiring a car. I can't drive, so you will have to drive, of course. That is if you're not too tired."

George leant back in his chair, resignedly.

"I'm not tired at all, Ralph."

"That's terrific. The car's waiting outside. I had it brought here this morning."

George was driving fast along steep, winding roads deep in the Yorkshire Dales. He had pulled himself together and could now focus on keeping Ralph happy at all times. The sun had come out of the clouds. In the distance up in the rolling hills, Bolton Castle was totally visible. But now Ralph was looking a little green.

"What's the matter, Ralph?" asked George.

"I'm feeling a little off-colour, George," answered Ralph, shakily. "Please could you stop the car."

George pulled over onto the verge and braked. Ralph immediately grabbed the door handle and fell out of the car. He headed to a spot behind it. George got out as well and walked over to him. Ralph was bending over, near the hedge.

"I am so sorry about this, George," he said when he finally stood up. "I couldn't help it. I thought I'd got over my car sickness."

"Are you feeling better now, Ralph?" asked George, sympathetically.

"Oh, much. But I'm not sure I want to get back into the car again. Could we just walk up to the castle, do you think?"

"Sure, Ralph," said George. It was only a mile away, and uphill. Bolton Castle turned out to be half in ruins. Ralph took George on a standard tour of the castle.

George was bored but was becoming good at not showing it.

Ralph wanted to go home by bus. "I feel better on buses, George," he said. But then he seemed to remember George's impending Court hearing and the sore memories that a bus might evoke. So he agreed to get back in the car and even managed not to be sick all the way back to Carshalton.

"I won't be hiring a car again, George," said Ralph, as they finally drew up at the Hall. "I'm sorry, George."

"Don't worry about it, Ralph," said George. "I'm getting quite accustomed to walking." This was true. He was.

The morning of the Magistrate's Court hearing had finally arrived. Always his true friend, Ralph accompanied him to Thirsk, and sat on the bench behind him, listening attentively to every word of the proceedings. Finally the Magistrate spoke directly to George. "Stand up," he said. George obeyed. "I believe that your actions were wholly intentional and routine. You are precisely the sort of fare evader that the Justice system endeavours to punish. You are fined four hundred and fifty pounds or two months in prison."

George just could not believe it. But he quickly recovered. As he had suspected would happen, Ralph came to the rescue and paid the fine upfront. As they stood outside the Magistrates Court in the warm June sunshine, George decided that things could not have gone better. There was, of course, the criminal record to consider, but George wasn't too worried. His future did not depend upon him having a pristine past.

Ralph wanted to go straight back to Carshalton, but

George felt like a drink in town. "I've been through a lot, Ralph," he said. Ralph reluctantly agreed. They walked along the road beside the noisy, busy traffic and into the Market Place then into a pub. Ralph said he didn't like the smoky atmosphere. So they went out again, and into the Black Bull, which was less crowded. After a beer and a chicken salad lunch, Ralph began to relax a bit more. At one time he even admitted to enjoying himself.

"It's nice to be out and about, George," he said.

"Out and about is overestimated," said George.

"It depends who you're out and about with," said Ralph.

Afterwards they went into the Black Swan, for another beer. Then into the Blacksmith's Arms, then the Royal Hotel. Ralph had drunk along with George the whole time and was starting to feel dizzy and excited. He was now talking in long stretches about many things. They fell out of the pub and into the Market Place again, and began to wander along, turning into Finkle Street. As they walked towards the old bridge, in the street halfway down there was another pub on the left, by the name of Ye Olde Three Tuns, which they had not yet been into. Without hesitation they went in there. George walked up to the bar to buy the drinks, and Ralph rounded a corner to find himself in a secluded back area. He sat down there, at a copper-topped table, alone. He could hear the subdued conversation and music coming from the front area.

A working-class man suddenly appeared, but it wasn't George. He sat down at the table next to Ralph's and got out a crumpled packet of cigarettes. Ralph felt annoyed. The man lit up, and clouds of smoke drifted over towards him. The man did not even seem to be trying to point his cigarette away from Ralph, who looked at him in disgust. But as Ralph continued to stare, the man turned briefly towards him, without much interest. Ralph was feeling more extrovert and charming than usual. He spoke.

"Excuse me," he said. "Could you do me a favour?"

The man looked at him, this time in the eyes. He seemed tired and depressed.

"Would you mind moving to the front area? Smoke bothers me."

The man laughed, as though this were a ridiculous suggestion, but didn't answer. Ralph felt agitated and frustrated.

"You must place a very low value on the quality of your life," said Ralph, with irritation. "To throw it away as you are doing"

"Oh, I believe in quality of life," said the man, in a strong accent which Ralph could not identify.

"Well, you have no reverence for life."

"Oh, I have reverence for life."

"Smokers don't have reverence for life."

The man did not answer. Eventually, he seemed to be coming to the end of his cigarette. He stubbed out what remained of it in the ash tray provided.

"I take it you have a very low opinion of people who smoke," he said.

"Yes, I do. They all have the same personality."

"No, they don't. That's like saying that all people who eat spaghetti Bolognese have the same personality."

Ralph considered this and decided that possibly there was an analogy.

"Smokers are psychopaths," he said.

The man laughed again. Then to Ralph's horror, he reached for the packet again. But this time, after he had lit up, Ralph decided that he had had enough. He reached over and took the cigarette from the man's very mouth, then stubbed it out in his own ash tray. But the next moment the man was grabbing him around the throat, and in a loud, rough voice, was demanding answers to abusive questions. Ralph thought he felt something in his neck crack. Then George suddenly appeared, carrying two beers. Just the sight of him approaching sent the man scurrying out the back door. George ran after him, but the man had already disappeared down an alleyway opposite, and George really couldn't be bothered to chase him. He went back into the pub to attend to Ralph.

"What on earth happened there, Ralph?" said George, sounding concerned.

"I only asked him to stop smoking," said Ralph. "When he wouldn't, I stubbed his cigarette out for him. Then he started going mental and grabbed my neck. It feels strange now," he went on, feeling it gingerly. "Like I might have broken a vertebra."

George moved one of the pints of beer towards Ralph, who began to drink immediately

"We'd better get you to a hospital," said George.

"Oh, no, I hate hospitals. I think it'll probably be all right."

"There might be something that needs seeing to now, Ralph," said George.

"I'll go later."

"Later might be too late."

However, Ralph really didn't want to go to the hospital. So they sat in the pub for another couple of hours, Ralph probing his neck every now and again. Finally they left the premises and found a taxi in the market square. George opened the door for Ralph. Throughout the journey back to Carshalton, Ralph stared straight ahead of him and was very quiet.

Back at the Hall, George was pleased to note that Lady Pulleine had gone to bed. He and Ralph walked into the drawing-room adjoining the dining room for a nightcap.

"You look as though you need a drink, Ralph," said George, pouring him a whisky from the drinks tray. Ralph sat down in his usual red leather armchair. He still appeared quite shaken.

"My neck still hurts," he said, feeling it tentatively.

"Well, I hope you've learnt your lesson, Ralph," said George.

"What's my lesson?"

"Never leave Carshalton Hall." Ralph looked at him with a distressed expression. George laughed impulsively. "I'm only kidding, Ralph. And I'm sure that neck injury isn't serious. If it still hurts tomorrow, we'll call a doctor."

It was two a.m. by the time they went to bed. However, George was awoken later in the night by raised voices, then became aware that it was Ralph, arguing with his mother. She had apparently found out about Ralph's injury and was up in arms about it.

"You're talking as though it was George's fault," shouted Ralph. "If it hadn't been for him, I could be dead now."

"You should have gone to the hospital," rasped the

mother, apparently changing the subject. Then their voices became quieter and gradually tailed off until they were out of earshot. George fell back to sleep again.

CHAPTER 9

The next morning dawned grey. Ralph was subdued, but not traumatised. George brought him breakfast in bed.

"How are you today, Ralph?"

Ralph attempted to sit up, then thought better of it.

"I've got a terrible hangover, George," he said. "My head feels like it's going to burst."

"Well, what do you expect, Ralph? You're unused to drinking."

Ralph glanced blearily at the breakfast tray. "I might be able to manage the orange juice," he said, trying to sit up again, and finally half-succeeding. George plumped up the pillows.

"It's a screwdriver," he said.

"Oh. Are you sure that's a good idea, George?"

"Yes. It'll cure your hangover. It's called 'hair of the dog.' "

Ralph reached out for the glass and nearly knocked it over. George handed it to him, and Ralph gulped the pale orange liquid bravely down. Then he took a bite from the piece of toast lying on the plate on the tray. But that was all he could manage, and his head then fell sideways again onto the pillow.

"I really think I need to go back to sleep again, George," he said. "I'm sorry."

"Don't worry," said George. "I'll look in on you later."

He picked up the tray and placed it on the dresser, then left the room, quietly closing the door behind him. He personally did not have a hangover. He was about to enter the dining room for breakfast, but through the partially open door, could see the mother sitting there, so went back to his room and waited.

At noon, he went to check on Ralph again. Ralph was still in bed. However, he appeared to be alive and awake. He even greeted George with a cheerful hello.

"I think that the hair of the dog worked, George," he said, sitting up, this time without any trouble at all. "I feel almost all right, now."

George smiled and walked over to him. "That's because you started drinking early," he explained. "The main part of the hangover occurred whilst you were asleep."

"Oh. That's neat, George."

"What about your neck?"

Ralph immediately felt it.

"Better. Yes, I think it is just a superficial neck injury, George. I don't need you to call the doctor."

"Good," said George.

"I've something to tell you, George," said Ralph, purposefully. "I'm changing my will."

"Oh, really," said George, politely.

"Yes. I don't think there's much point leaving Carshalton Hall to my cousin. I hardly know her, and in any case, she's got enough money of her own already. I was only following mother's instructions. And considering the way mother speaks to me, I don't think that she deserves my obedience."

"But who else can you leave it to, Ralph? Some yet more distant relative?"

"I don't know any yet more distant relatives. No, George, I'm leaving it to you. Not that you will outlive me. I've got to have a will," he added hurriedly.

"Well, that's very nice, Ralph," said George.

"So you'll always have somewhere to live," concluded Ralph, happily. "I know you couldn't go back to council accommodation after living here. I certainly couldn't."

"I'd agree with that," said George. "But what about your mother? Where would she live?"

"She will continue to have right of occupancy."

"Oh," said George. Ralph observed his expression.

"I know you don't get on with her," said Ralph. "She doesn't understand you. Not that she understands me. She's never understood me." Ralph looked sad again.

More days passed. It was now only three weeks until Ralph's twenty-first birthday. George was starting to feel stressed again. He was now on the will, but would he stay on it? Did the mother know he was on it? Possibly not. He dared not ask. George had not bothered to buy Ralph birthday presents. He could not afford it, and Ralph knew that he could not afford it. He was still wearing Ralph's dead father's clothes. If only they weren't just that bit too large for him. Perhaps when Ralph came into his money, he might become more generous. But Rose had told him that the money amounted to only about a quarter of a million. Hardly enough for a young man about town to live off the interest, as Ralph was presently doing. A nasty thought struck him. Ralph had not mentioned leaving him any money in his new will. Well, thought George, I'm not greedy. Perhaps I could be content with just the Hall.

CHAPTER 10

It was Ralph's twenty-first birthday. Ralph had toyed with the idea of having a party, but George had talked him out of it. For one thing, he had pointed out, for a party, you needed guests. How many people did Ralph know, let alone could invite? Apart from the servants, there were very few people who could possibly be invited. Short of bringing in people from The Stanwick Arms, or the telephone directory, there really was no one that Ralph could invite. Ralph had finally seen the logic in this and decided not to have a party, which pleased George no end. The last thing he wanted was for Ralph to be conversing with people from the outside world. They might put negative ideas into his head, such as questioning the suitability of his current companion.

So instead of a party, Ralph was to have a birthday tea, attended by George and his mother, and possibly some of the servants.

That afternoon, George had been on his best behaviour. At one point the mother had even smiled at him. Things really were going quite well for him at Carshalton Hall. The mother's presents to Ralph consisted of various self-help books and colourful clothes. She appeared to have spent a good few hundred pounds on him. But Ralph was not that appreciative. He had the air of someone who had expected nothing and got nothing. George was glad when the mother finally retired to her private suite of rooms.

"How does it feel to have full control over Carshalton Hall?" asked George, finally, sitting back in the dining room chair.

"Oh, no different from before. I haven't really thought about it."

But George had certainly thought about it. There was now a very real possibility that he could become the sole owner of Carshalton Hall. However, it would look too suspicious if this happened too soon after Ralph's twenty-first birthday.

"Though, I am starting to feel more independent," said Ralph. "Thinking for myself and making my own decisions. Like changing my will, for example. And another thing I've realised is that mother isn't always right."

"Well, she has to be right sometimes, Ralph," said George. "Nobody is always wrong."

Ralph pondered over this. "Yes, she's probably right about twenty-five percent of the time," he said, with concentration. "But I feel unduly influenced by her."

"Well, everybody is influenced by their parents," said George. "It isn't a sign of weakness."

"Well, I feel weak," said Ralph. "At least, I used to."

"Well, at least you're a lot richer now, Ralph," said George. "You've got money to spend."

"I can't spend the capital," said Ralph, anxiously. "I'll end up ruined."

"You're already ruined."

"Perhaps I should sell the Hall," pondered Ralph.

George did not like that idea. Carshalton Hall was his heirloom.

"Don't do anything rash with the house," he said. "You will always need somewhere to live."

"Yes, perhaps you're right, George."

After tea had finally reached the end of its course, Ralph wanted to play cards again. They were still playing with draughts for chips. Sitting at the dining room table, George dealt, using a new pack of cards. He had decided to let Ralph win. With a useless hand, he re-raised several times on the river, and Ralph called his bluff.

"I knew I could beat you eventually, George," he crowed, turning over pocket aces. The board had not helped George's eight-three offsuit. With both hands, Ralph raked in the large pile of draughts.

George smiled. "I think you're good enough to play for money, now Ralph," he said. "Now that you've come into some."

But for some reason, Ralph did not seem as keen on the idea as he usually was. "I made the decision a long time ago that when I came into my money, I wouldn't gamble a penny of it," he said. "And I'm going to stick to that."

"Right you are, Ralph," said George, collecting up the cards. "I guess there isn't really any point in continuing, then."

At breakfast the next morning, George brought up the delicate subject of money again.

"It must be nice having money to spend now, Ralph," he began. "You were roughing it a bit, before."

Ralph looked up from his scrambled eggs, knife and fork in hand.

"It doesn't make any difference," he said, looking straight ahead of him. "As I said yesterday, I can't spend the capital. I shall continue to live on just the interest, as before."

Ralph appeared to have inherited his mother's parsimonious streak. George was still collecting both housing and incapacity benefit; as well as this he was also subletting his flat in Walworth to an associate. Living at Carshalton meant that he did not need to buy any domestic necessities. However, he had been hoping that on reaching his twenty-first birthday, Ralph would be able to provide him with a few luxuries. But it was not to be, so it would seem.

"Aren't you going to treat yourself to anything?"

"No," replied Ralph, again without looking at him.

George now felt sure that he was not in line for any of the money, either now, or on the will. He told himself that this did not matter.

CHAPTER II

As the autumnal weeks passed, Ralph's meanness continued to be prevalent. George's expectations of a whole new wardrobe for himself had still not materialised, not to mention the various toys that he had hoped Ralph would wish to purchase, once he was in the money. Absolutely nothing had changed. What was worse was that Ralph was still expecting him to trek around Yorkshire on foot with him almost everyday. On one afternoon they had been walking back from viewing some most interesting archaeological remains some five miles north from Carshalton.

"You know, Ralph, the life we lead here really is no different to that of two eighteenth century gentlemen," observed George.

"You're right," agreed Ralph. "I often remind myself of Ralph Thoresby, who lived near here in the early eighteenth century and wrote a diary. It was printed in book form some time during the nineteenth century. We have a copy of it in the new library."

"Oh. What sort of things did he write about?"

"Oh, about riding out and discovering things in the local area. Like, for example, viewing the vestigia of a lately discovered Roman town, with the remains of the aquaduct, pillars and monuments. Though I don't think the diary would particularly interest you, George. It is not exactly an 'action' diary.

"There aren't any juicy bits?"

"Well, he does mention something about Mr Busby hanging from a gibbet," said Ralph. "He seemed quite pleased about it. Actually, on second thoughts, I don't think I would like to meet Ralph Thoresby," he went on in his frequently used ponderous tone. "He sounds a bit sanctimonious."

George sat down in a relaxed fashion on a nearby tree stump.

"What you really need to get around Yorkshire with is a motorcycle," said George. "Or a moped, at least. You wouldn't need a licence for that."

"They sound dangerous, George," objected Ralph.

"Oh, not really, Ralph. Most accidents are caused by somebody doing something stupid."

Ralph sat down beside him. "Well, I'm perfectly capable of doing something stupid, George," he said. "There was a boy at my school who was killed in a motorcycle accident. Though he wasn't actually riding the motorcycle. He was in the side car."

"Well, I'm not suggesting we get one of those, Ralph," said George. He stared out into the distance. Ralph said nothing

"They're really not very expensive, Ralph," he cajoled. "A couple of motorbikes certainly wouldn't break your bank balance."

"Well, I suppose they could be rather fun, in a way," said Ralph. He was now clearly imagining himself, seated on a motorbike, speeding through the Yorkshire countryside. That was encouraging.

"They are enormous fun, Ralph," confirmed George.

But two weeks later, Ralph did a U-turn on the motor-bikes idea. At breakfast one morning, he said that he had had, as he put it, a 'rethink'. George felt exasperated but managed not to show any such feeling.

"Well, it's up to you, of course, Ralph," he said, without encouragement, then dropped the subject.

It was one of the few awkward, unpleasant occasions when George was obliged to dine with the mother present, as she was apt to occasionally be. Rose, however, was not serving. When Ralph asked the mother why this was, she replied in her usual harsh and haughty tone that Hippolita had gone, and would not return. George looked up abruptly from his meal. "What's happened to Rose?" he queried.

"She is expecting a child," said the mother, in a dis-approving tone. "And she blames you."

"What?" gasped George.

Ralph's expression was even more surprised. He immediately put down his desert spoon and shoved the plate aside.

"Oh, that's ridiculous, mother. How could it possibly be George? He hardly has anything to do with Rose." Ralph then quickly looked at George, in a slightly worried fashion.

"It's almost certainly not me," said George, in response.

"What do you mean, almost?" asked Ralph, aghast.

George stopped eating momentarily. "It's unlikely to be me, Ralph," he said, in repetition. "I don't have an interest in Rose," he added, then continued to eat.

Ralph appeared somewhat disturbed and was silent for the rest of the meal. However, George felt compelled to ask the mother a further question.

"What's she doing for money?"

"Hippolita is not working, now. I have found her a flat."

"You're subsidising her?"

"Yes. When you have servants, you have a responsibility towards them."

On hearing this, George decided to try and forget about the matter.

The days dragged on. It was strange that weeks and months could pass without events or memories. At one time it had been September, now it was March. It was all a boring blur. The only thing that George could remember as happening clearly during that time was Christmas Day. For this special occasion, Ralph had condescended to release some of his capital and direct it towards George in the form of a cheque for two hundred pounds. George considered that this was less than one ten-thousandth of Ralph's entire wealth.

"Thank you very much, Ralph," he had said, on opening the Christmas card containing the cheque. "You're a good friend."

"I think I've been a bit selfish, George," Ralph had returned. "You really are quite strapped for cash, aren't you George?"

"You can say that again," George had answered fervently.

The whole winter at Carshalton had been a pretty

miserable affair. The mother had spent most of the time curled up in a rug in the morning room, watching television. That suited George fine, but the dead, freezing atmosphere both inside and outside the house was getting to him. It also seemed to be getting to the old, oak tree at the edge of the lawn, which appeared petrified and lifeless but would undoubtedly revive miraculously in the spring. An indeed, already by the end of February, something resembling spring, with leaves but no buds on the trees, and the sound of sheep bleating in the fields had begun to pervade the scene. George and Ralph were out and about again. As they walked along the main road to Caldwell, in the fresh, reviving air, George was alarmed to observe that Ralph's step appeared to be unusually sprightly.

"I've been thinking of turning Carshalton Hall into an hotel," said Ralph, energetically. "It could make quite an expensive hotel. Five stars, at least."

"Are you sure you want to do that, Ralph?" asked George, at once. "It sounds like a major undertaking."

"I realise that," said Ralph, ponderously. "But I think I could manage it. I have always wanted to live in an hotel."

"Well, it's up to you, Ralph," said George. "If you think you can cope with a load of strangers in your house." Ralph did not appear deflated.

"Oh no, they would be company for me," he said.

Then about a week later, another worrying event occurred. George had come down late for breakfast, and unusually, the door to the mother's suite of rooms was wide open, allowing George to look into a neat, refurbished corridor with a mirror and side table, upon which was placed a vase of fresh flowers. The mother seemed to be living remarkably well in there. No wonder she did not give a damn about the rest of the house. But the most alerting thing of all was the sound of raised voices, coming from somewhere within. George identified them immediately as being that of Ralph and the mother. It was an agitated conversation which reminded him of the one that she and Ralph had held in the morning room the day after he first arrived at Carshalton, only this time he could hear every word. As before, it concerned himself.

"He thinks he is onto a good thing here," the mother was saying, loudly and clearly. "Free board and lodging. And he is probably illegally renting out his council flat."

"Not probably. I know for a fact that he is. He told me."

"I am not sure I approve of that."

"He's not as rich as you, mother. If he isn't living there, he has to rent it out."

"At a higher rate than he is paying, I presume."

"Well, why not?"

"He is the last person I would want my son to be associating with."

"You don't know him."

"I don't want to know him. I think he could be dangerous. For all you know, he may have been in prison. Has he ever had a job?"

"Not that I know of."

"I do wish you would tell him to go, Ralph."

"I'll think about it."

George could hear Ralph's quick, light footsteps approaching and hurriedly moved out of sight. He went into the dining room and sat down on a chair at the circular table. A moment later, Ralph joined him. He appeared somewhat flushed.

"How are you today, Ralph?" asked George, as the young man sat down. He had the appearance of someone who had just been in an arranged car accident.

"Oh, all right. I just had a long, stressful conversation with mother. She keeps going on about sending you packing."

"Oh, dear. Well, I'll go if you want me to, Ralph. I can always go back to my flat."

"No, don't worry, George. I can handle mother." Ralph began buttering a piece of toast in a concentrated fashion, then poured himself coffee. Unlike George, he usually drank tea. As he ate, he grinned briefly at George in a slightly anxious fashion. "Chill out, Ralph," said George, in response. "Be cool."

But George also felt perturbed. Was he losing control? Supposing that Ralph couldn't handle mother. Supposing she got through to him one day.

George was now as familiar with the Hall as Ralph himself was, if not more familiar, for he still had not informed Ralph of the existence of the secret door in the Gallery. He had had no reason to do so. They were sitting in the drawing-room reading the Sunday magazines, an activity which prior to his arrival at Carshalton, George had held in total contempt. However, the publication through which he was now languidly browsing was not completely without interest. An article pertaining to body language had caught his attention. Apparently, two people in conversation often adopted identical postures.

This was especially true in the case of close friends and lovers. Were he to stand upstairs on the second floor of the West Wing, leaning against the banister, was it not possible that Ralph would do the same? Though of course, Ralph would be leaning against the part of the banister that was about to give way. George decided to tell Ralph about the secret staircase. He put down the magazine.

Ralph was pretending to read the Sunday Observer. George looked in his direction, but Ralph continued to stare at the pages. Finally, George spoke.

"Did you know that there is a secret staircase at Carshalton Hall?"

Ralph immediately put down the newspaper.

"I doubt it, George."

"Oh, but there is. Would you like me to show you?"

"Certainly."

George stood up, and they walked out of the breakfast room together. "It starts in the Gallery, behind the large tapestry, and leads up to the storeroom floor above," said George. Ralph was very surprised when George showed him the door in the oak panelling through which the staircase could be accessed.

"Why have I never seen this before?" he complained.

"You're not inquisitive enough, Ralph," said George.

"No, I suppose you're right. I should take more notice of what is going on around me." He stuck his head into the dark area beyond and sneezed.

"Ralph, I have to go to the toilet," said George.

"Oh. All right, George, I'll see you in a minute." Ralph watched ponderously as George walked quickly away and out of the Gallery. Then without further hesitation, he stepped in, advancing awkwardly upwards to the top; there he discovered the door. In wondrous anticipation, he pushed it open and stepped into the storeroom. The gaping hole in the roof had still not yet been repaired, and daylight streamed into the darkness. A dead pigeon, fallen through, lay morbidly upon the worn and rotting floorboards. Ralph had had every intention to attend to the damage, but somehow the matter had slipped into the background of his thoughts. Only now was he truly reminded of it.

George really had needed to go to the toilet. He had briefly returned to his room in the East Wing but was back through the oak door five minutes later. He crossed through the Blue Drawing-room and into the hallway of the West Wing, where he could hear Ralph clumping around on the second floor. He stood at the spot which lay directly underneath the dodgy banister.

"Are you up there, Ralph?" he called out, in a loud voice.

Ralph appeared up above. "Where are you, George?" he answered, looking around. "I can't see you. Are you downstairs?" A moment later he leant over the banister. It immediately creaked and gave way; together with broken rails and pieces of three hundred-year-old wood, Ralph fell head first to the ground below and lay there motionless, his body in a distorted position. As George observed him, something almost resembling remorse passed briefly through his mind. He felt almost responsible. No one had apparently heard the thump, no one came running. Stepping around the body, George walked straight back into the East Wing. The first person he encountered was Gertrude, and he told her the terrible news. After that it was no longer necessary for him to do anything or inform anybody; everything happened automatically. An ambulance was called, but when it arrived it turned out that Ralph was without any doubt dead. The police would have to be called. Unable to take anymore, George went up to his room.

A little later, watching through the latticed windows, he saw a police car draw up at the door. George felt slightly nervous. He walked out onto the upper landing and heard quietly spoken voices as Gertrude led three uniformed police officers through to the West Wing. There he hung around until two of them returned. Looking over the banisters, he could see Gertrude showing them into the drawing-room in which he knew that the mother was already sitting. He was glad he could not hear the ensuing conversation; no doubt it would be unbearably painful to listen to. Then the moment that he had been dreading finally arrived: Gertrude emerged from the room and called out to him, aware that he was hovering somewhere upstairs. George went straight down.

As he entered the neat and elegant room, he was observed by all present. He was invited to sit down in the seat opposite the red armchair where Ralph usually sat, but which was now occupied by a uniformed man with a steely stare. George was initially intimidated but then felt annoyed. Technically, he told himself, he had done nothing wrong.

"I take it you were quite friendly with Ralph," the man began.

"I suppose you could say that," said George.

The man refused to take his eyes off him and appeared

to be closely observing his demeanour. George was also aware of the other, younger policeman seated with a notepad in a neighbouring chair and apparently required only to listen and write. George gave him occasional glances. He felt calm now. At first, he was able to answer all questions smoothly and satisfactorily. But at one point they took an awkward turn and began to focus on his housing and employment status.

"Were you working before you came here?"

"No. I suffer from clinical depression and have been on incapacity benefit for six years."

"That must be awful."

"Yes, it is."

"Could I take your address in London, please."

"Yes. 415 Leicester Place, Walworth, SE1"

He watched as all this was written down by the non-speaking police officer. George hoped that the man would get the details down wrong, though the idea that he might be about to lose the flat did not, in the circumstances, concern him greatly. However, he was glad when the questions were turned in the mother's direction. Despite the requests for detail, all she seemed able to manage was a faltering yes or no. The senior officer had a melancholy look about him, as though he was not happy with the way in which the interview was going. He kept looking around him as if he were hoping to glean some extra information from the surroundings. George felt slightly worried.

The front entrance bell rang out suddenly throughout the house. Gertrude got up immediately and left the room; presently he could hear her voice and others. George remained seated as the two officers walked out into the hallway, leaving him alone with the mother. She had appeared previously to be in a state of mental breakdown but now seemed surprisingly together, and was staring at him with an expression of pure hatred, as though he himself were responsible for Ralph's tragic death. George looked back at her and crossed his legs. A silence ensued.

"I didn't kill him," he said finally.

"You killed him as surely as if you had pointed a gun to his head."

George stood up.

"You will leave this house immediately," said the mother. "Go."

George regarded her in a mockingly apologetic fashion.

"I hate to tell you this, but this is my house now. Or at least, it will be very soon. Ralph changed his will."

The mother regarded him with an expression of stone.

"The money as well?"

"No. Just the house."

"You won't get either. Life imprisonment is what you will get."

George regarded the ceiling in a bored fashion.

"The entire West Wing is an accident waiting to happen," he pointed out, wearily. "I nearly broke my neck slipping on that stair carpet. You're lucky I didn't sue you."

The mother seemed unable to respond to this, so George took the opportunity to make his exit. Another, uniformed officer with four bands on either sleeve was standing in the hallway, listening to the account of his inferiors. George stepped discreetly across to the staircase and was about to ascend when he heard a man's voice behind him.

"Just a minute, Sir."

George turned patiently round to face the uniformed officer with the bands. More tedious questions awaited him.

"Superintendent Rales."

"Hello," said George.

"I gather you actually saw the accident."

"Yes," responded George, readily. "He fell headfirst from the second floor of the West Wing. No one could have survived that."

"Where were you at the time?"

"In the hallway of the West Wing. I had just gone to the toilet."

"And he fell just as you came back into the hallway."

"Yes, more or less."

The Superintendent got out a notebook and pencil. "We may require you for further questioning," he said, writing something down. "So we would appreciate it if you could make yourself available to us over the coming weeks."

"Certainly."

George was allowed to go upstairs. But sensing that going upstairs might be regarded as a little suspect or odd, he changed his mind and went into the dining room instead. Feeling the need for air, he stepped out through the French windows onto the short lawn at the back of the house and wandered down the field to the beck, hoping to relieve the vertiginous feeling of disorientation that was affecting him. It was still light but the orange sun was low down in the trees, and the air was rather cold. He strolled along beside the beck, towards the woodland and back again. Sometime later, he did not know how long, he stood at the bottom of the field, facing the house. A middle-aged man in a shabby raincoat was approaching him across the grass. What now, thought George, realizing that the man was probably yet another member of the police force. George stood with his hands in his pockets, watching the man until he came right up to him, briefly holding up ID and introducing himself as Detective Sergeant something or other. Just like on the television, thought George.

"They told me you would be out here," said the man in a deceptively casual tone of voice. "I just want to ask you a couple of questions."

"Sure," said George, unconcernedly. But he didn't quite like the way the man was looking at him.

"How long did you say you'd lived here?"

"Oh, less than a year. I met Ralph in May last year."

"Where exactly did you meet him?"

"In the church nearby. The church of Stanwick St John."

"Do you often visit churches?"

"No." George was starting to feel really tired. The man in the raincoat seemed to notice this, for he said:

"We can go inside and sit down if you like, sir."

"No, I'm all right," said George. "It's just the shock, that's all. I just can't believe what's happened."

"Well, that's what we're here for," said the Detective Sergeant. "To find out exactly what did happen."

George glanced perturbedly at the man.

"And more importantly, to find out why it happened. Forensics should help to tell us that."

"Forensics?"

"Yes. A forensic team is on its way now."

George said nothing.

"It's quite a nice place, this," said the man, gazing out at the meadows and woodland beyond the beck. "I wouldn't mind living here myself. Though I suppose after a while, I might start to get extremely bored."

"You're absolutely right," said George.

"We may need you again to help in our enquiries," the Detective went on. "I presume you will continue to reside here for the time being."

"You presume correctly," said George.

"And as the key witness, you will be required to give evidence at the inquest."

"Will there be an inquest?"

"Oh, yes. There is always an inquest when the cause of death is unnatural."

George had forgotten about inquests. "That's not a trial, is it?" he asked, anxiously.

"No. It is merely an inquiry."

George felt sick. "When will the inquest take place?" he asked, faintly.

"Oh, about six to twelve weeks from now, I should think."

It was after midnight when the police finally all left. Ralph's body had been removed, and apart from the banister up above, dramatically broken away, everything was as before. A sort of peaceful aftermath reigned over the house, now in a dark shadow. George had recovered himself to some degree; as he ambled up the dimly lit staircase to the guest room, he began to consider his future life at Carshalton Hall. There were three things that he intended to do in the fairly immediate future: the first would be to buy some new clothes. The second, to change his name by deed-poll to George Pulleine. And thirdly, he intended to put up a monument to Catherine Pulleine in the church of Stanwick-St-John.

CHAPTER 12

On getting up the following morning, George was slightly put out to discover that nobody was in the kitchen. He would be obliged to fix his own breakfast. Unaccustomed to this it was with irritation that he walked around the spacious culinary area trying to find cups, saucers and fresh bread. To his relief, however, Gertrude eventually appeared. Her maid's uniform was crumpled, her red hair with the grey roots dishevelled and her mood, instead of mildly uncertain and polite, appeared nervous and depressed.

"Ah, there you are," said George. "I was wondering where you'd got to."

Gertrude walked tiredly over to the stove. "I've been with Lady Pulleine half the night," she said, without looking at him. "She's beside herself. It took a few hours to hit her."

"Well, I suppose it would do," said George, sitting down at the kitchen table. "Losing her only son."

Gertrude did not respond. She appeared to be in the process of making the mother's usual breakfast. "Don't bother with mine," said George, helpfully.

"I wasn't going to." Gertrude placed a saucepan carelessly onto a hob. "Madam told me that you are to become the official head of household," she added, apparently on an afterthought.

George put his feet up on one of the other wooden chairs. "That's right," he confirmed. "That was what Ralph wanted."

"It's not what Madam wanted. She's not happy about that at all. She wasn't even aware of it until just now."

"Are you happy about it?"

"It's not my place to be happy or unhappy about it."

George picked up the plate of toast and cup of tea and walked out. He sat in the dining room and stared out at the trees and beck at the end of the field. It could be a little while before Ralph's solicitors contacted him. Fortunately they, and not the mother, were the executors of Ralph's will. But supposing the mother contested the will? There was also another potential problem; although Ralph had promised him the Hall, he had said nothing of its contents. Without them, there would be nothing to sell and therefore no income. There was, of course, the set of 'Characteristicks,' which Ralph had officially given him, but for sentimental reasons, George was as reluctant to sell that as he would be to sell the Hall. However, he was fairly sure that no catalogue of the books in the Old Library existed thereby making it impossible for anyone to prove that any particular book had ever been there. Not that anyone would ever notice if a book went missing. The mother never set foot in the West Wing, and Gertrude never entered the Old Library. There was also the 'Boulle' writing desk, as Ralph had called it, in the West Sitting room. Ralph claimed to have inherited it at birth. Who was to say that Ralph had not given this to him? Though in less than perfect condition, it might fetch a couple of thousand or maybe even twenty thousand. He had no idea. George felt a little more encouraged. But then a nasty thought struck him. Ralph's behaviour towards him had changed slightly in the last few weeks. Supposing the guy had had one of his 'rethinks' and had at the last minute struck off his loyal companion from the will. He would be thrown out of Carshalton Hall within days, without a penny to his name. What was more, judging from his recent interview with the police he was about to lose the flat in Walworth. In the worst case, he would be in a very short while homeless, for at least a temporary period. Leaving the empty plate and cup upon the table, George left the room.

For the first time since arriving at Carshalton, he went back to the Old Library in the West Wing. No doubt 'Characteristicks' was not the only first edition in good condition. He needed to identify what was there. The dust was worse than ever. For the first time ever, George coughed. I'm getting as bad as Ralph, he thought, as he ran his hand along the spines of the old volumes lining the lengthy mahogany shelves. Some were broken or hanging off threads. He made a mental note of where the less dog-eared volumes were placed; some of them were first editions. A silver inkstand on an upper shelf which he had not previously noticed also caught his attention; but it was probably worth no more than a few hundred pounds.

As he wandered back through the empty, spacious, dust-ridden rooms of the West Wing, he realised that he was completely at a loss as to what to do. Until Ralph's solicitor contacted him the situation was frozen; he was in limbo. One thing was however certain; he had no wish to encounter the mother at any time during the next six weeks. As he came through into the East Wing again, he could hear her voice, insistent and wailing, echoing throughout the Hall. He decided to go out.

With only a jumper for warmth, he felt rather cold as he strolled around Carshalton. However, there was no wind. The snow had melted a fortnight ago, and the beck was running noisily again. He hopped over the flat stepping stones that lead to the field on the other side and continued on. The north side of Carshalton Wood lay beyond. He wondered if all this would soon be his, or would it just be the Hall. As he approached the scantily leaved trees, he wondered if the mother was watching him from the morning room. He recollected the day in May on which she had spotted him emerging from the trees. Why did the woman have to exist?

When he reached the outskirts of the wood, he went for a long, aimless walk all around the area, through small, lifeless villages, fields of cows, sheep, stony grassland, short grass, long grass. By early evening he still had not regained his composure. As he walked back in through the black door with the polished handle, he was not sure if anyone was around.

The dining table did not appear to be laid for dinner. George walked into the kitchen to find out why. Gertrude was not there, but Cook was standing at the stove, stirring some kind of stew. She did not look at him.

"Excuse me," said George, politely. "What time is dinner?"

"Lady Pulleine is 'avin' dinner on a tray in the drawing-room," she answered after a moment, in a surly fashion.

"Where am I having dinner?"

"I didn't know you was 'avin' dinner."

"Well, I am."

"Well, I suppose I could bring somethin' through to you. You'll have to lay the table yourself, though."

What a drag, thought George. But he knew where everything was.

"I'd like a bottle of Chardonnay to go with the meal."

The cook did not answer. A little later, George was sitting at the table in the dining-room. From the adjoining drawing-room, he could hear the television. Presumably, the mother had taken up TV dinners. It was an uncomfortable feeling, knowing that only a thin wall separated them. After a while the cook plodded in, carrying a casserole, which she placed down heavily on the table.

"You'll have to fetch the veg yerself. I'm attendin' to my employer."

What would I be doing with veg, thought George. He served himself some of the casserole and began to eat. After dinner, he would go down to The Stanwick Arms. He wondered just how much the locals knew about recent events and whether or not their attitude towards him had changed. He was surely the subject of gossip. Hopefully, as the prospective new Squire, he would receive the reception that he deserved.

Half-an-hour later George headed off between the ghostly trees of Carshalton Wood. The branches waved in agitation as the wind was up, drowning out the nearby beck. He came out into the fields under a cloudy, starless sky. There was no moon. Buffeted along by the gale, he progressed through the dark towards the distant lights of Aldbrough. The air was distinctly chilly, and it was beginning to drizzle. As he crossed the old bridge, he glanced over its arched walls to see the stormy beck, rushing in agitation beneath him. The bay windows of The Stanwick Arms were lit up. He would be glad to get inside.

As George entered the white-framed glass doors, a few heads turned; the news of his inheritance had reached their ears. He approached the bar. The proprietor was leaning on the counter listening to a customer's monologue. George waited patiently. Finally, the proprietor turned expectantly towards him.

"A pint of Stella Artois." George placed the money on the counter. He felt as he had done that afternoon when he had first arrived at Carshalton.

The proprietor took the money without a word. The man had never been particularly chatty, but now he was being downright rude, thought George. At least he did not appear to be banned from The Stanwick Arms.

"How's business?" he asked, lamely.

"I'm not speaking to you," said the landlord and walked to the other end of the bar.

George went and sat down at the only vacant table by the window, the same table at which he had sat when he had first arrived. The village green was as dark and deserted as ever. Inside, what should have been the cosy interior had no warmth to it at all. Finally, he saw Derek entering the premises. He watched as the man bought a drink, expecting him to join him at his window table but instead he merely turned towards George, gave him a brief, "Hello," then walked to the far end of the room to talk to others. George downed the remainder of his beer and walked out.

Fifteen minutes later, George returned to Carshalton Hall for the second time that day. On both occasions he had half-expected the locks to have been changed, by order of Lady Pulleine. However, she appeared to have other things to think on. When he opened the front door, the hallway was in total darkness. As he switched on the dim lights and made his way towards the shallow stairway, George reassured himself that there had been no further visits from the police in the last twenty-four hours. Hopefully they were now regarding Ralph's death as nothing more than a tragic accident. He had six weeks to prepare himself for the impending inquest.

CHAPTER 13

George was rudely awakened the following morning by the sound of a lawnmower. As he was wrenched out of his sleep, it dawned on him that the early arrival of Spring had brought on a growth spurt in the grass of the front lawn. He got up immediately and went over to the window. Through the latticed panes, he could see Mr Stokes energetically driving up and down in straight lines that would put to shame the Lord's Cricket Ground. But why did it have to be done so early?

George donned the clothes that he had been wearing the day before, went downstairs and out the front entrance. It was a chilly morning, despite being Spring. He walked quickly over the gravel and onto the lawn, towards the mower. It seemed like the gardener was not going to stop, but then he did, within an inch of running George over.

"I say, would you mind doing this at a later time, in future?" began George, in a loud voice, despite the fact that the motor was no longer on. "It really is very disturbing when people are trying to sleep."

"You'll have to talk to Lady Pulleine about that," said the gardener, and abruptly moved off again, drowning George's objections with the noise of the motor. George stared after him, then walked back into the Hall. Well, he was up now. There was no point trying to go back to sleep. He would have breakfast, then attend to the remaining matters on his agenda. The paranoia that Ralph might have changed his will was gone, and everything seemed to be in order.

Half an hour later, he was hurrying off along the dirt track towards Aldbrough, a daunting walk when he first arrived but which really only took a quarter of an hour and was no bother at all. He desired to look into the possibility of placing a memorial to Catherine Pulleine on the north wall of the church of Stanwick-St-John. This necessitated the use of a telephone. The mother might discover his investigations on her itemised telephone bill, so it would be better use the nearest public call box instead of the one in the drawing-room. There was one on the village green, beside the bus shelter. Fortunately today it was in working order. The pub was not yet open. George got his notepad out and stepped into the cubicle. It had begun to drizzle.

After several calls, it turned out that putting up a memorial in a church was actually a lot more complicated than George had anticipated. First, it was necessary to provide proof of the person's existence. Then the Parochial Church Council would have to agree to the request for a memorial. The Parochial Church Council then had to apply to the Diocesan Registrar for a faculty. Then the Registrar would have to have the faculty approved by the Chancellor of the Dioceses. When George finally emerged from the phone box, it was raining in a persistent sort of manner.

George decided to get the wheels in motion. How

long would it take, he wondered? As he queued in the Post Office for stamps, he considered that there was a distinct possibility that he would be obstructed at some point by some obstinate member of the clergy. Back at the Hall, he sat at the 'Boulle' desk in the West Sitting Room, writing out in ink the initial letter to the Parochial Church Council on the nice letter paper that had been conveniently provided in the guest room, along with the mineral water and tea making facilities. It would, he reflected, be appropriate to commission some proper, headed letter paper for his future communications, to make it clear that they were coming from an important place. Not just letter paper; a general 'Carshalton Hall' stationery would be the order of the day. In fact, why stop at stationery? He would also need match boxes each with a miniature photograph of the building on one side and on the other a photograph of ... well, he would think of something. A personal wax seal might also not be a bad idea. After carefully folding the letter and placing it in an envelope, he wrote out the address, properly centered. He would have to do something about his handwriting. The Lord of the Manor should not be writing in a semi-illegible scrawl, like that of an illiterate. He would practice copying out of calligraphy books until he could write in the elegant, copperplate style of Catherine Pulleine. He placed a stamp meticulously in the top right-hand corner.

In an energetic step, George strode out of the Hall again, to post the important letter personally in the postbox on the main road. He was not going to entrust the task to any of the servants. The rain was letting up now and the sun hazy but visible. As he emerged from the woods, he was passed by a black car, turning in from the main road. Panic rose up within him. It was the police again, come to take him away. But as the car passed him, he considered that they must have seen him, and would have stopped, if they had had business with him. Perhaps it was not the police. Well, who then? Visitors for Lady Pulleine. The question as to whether those with Right of Occupancy were entitled to visitors raised itself in George's mind. It depended on the terms stipulated, he supposed. He did not want all and sundry walking in and out of the building the whole time.

On the walk back through Carshalton Wood, he encountered no one. But as he came out of the wood and onto the gravel surrounding the front lawn, the black car was there, visibly parked in front of the entrance to the East Wing. George quietly opened the front entrance door with the key that Ralph had given him some months ago and stepped furtively into the hallway. As he did so, Gertrude emerged from the kitchen area, carrying a tray of tea things. She appeared to be heading for the morning room.

"Oh, Gertrude, could you tell me who the visitors are?" he queried, as she passed him, rudely ignoring him. He watched as tediously, she placed the tea tray on a nearby table, opened the door to the morning room and picked up the tray again to carry it into the room. Someone closed the door closed behind her as she walked in. George sighed in exasperation. The servants had started behaving in a strangely uncooperative and hostile manner. George tried not to think about how the gardener had spoken to him that morning.

Later, strolling around down by the beck he caught

sight of Gertrude in the dining-room, polishing the table. George walked up the field at the back of the house and came in through the French windows.

"Could you make me a pot of coffee with cream, please?" asked George politely. "I'll have it in the drawing-room."

"I'm sorry, sir, I'm too busy. You'll have to make it yourself."

"Have Lady Pulleine's visitors gone?"

"Yes, sir."

"Who were they?"

"Undertakers for Ralph's funeral, sir."

"Oh, of course." In all the excitement, George had completed forgotten about Ralph's inevitable funeral. Presumably he would not be invited.

George walked through the door in the partition and into the drawing-room, where he sat down in Ralph's favourite red leather armchair and picked up the newspaper conveniently lying on the table, next to the mints and a decorative box of long matches which nobody ever used.

Unfolding the large pages, listlessly, he began to read. He would have to do something about the servants. The trouble was, it would appear that they were somehow associated with the mother's Right of Occupancy. He was probably stuck with them. In any case, he had no idea how to go about obtaining a new lot of servants. He put the matter temporarily out of his mind. Right now, he considered that he was not really in a position to make any changes and it was probably advisable that for the next six weeks he should keep a very low profile.

CHAPTER 14

In a bare room, George was seated at a table opposite the same non-uniformed officer whom he had had the pleasure of meeting three days earlier. Beside this man was another non-uniformed officer, presumably another Detective of some sort.

George was feeling tired again. Lying in his bed that morning in the guest room at Carshalton Hall he had been abruptly arrested by two uniforms 'on suspicion of murder', cautioned, bundled into a cage-like area at the back of a police vehicle and then, on arrival at the 'Custody Suite,' had been thrown into a cell for half and hour. Now he was being interviewed. He had not exercised his right to speak to a solicitor or consult the 'Codes of Practice' booklet made available to him. Why would an innocent person need to do either?

"We now have both the results of the post-mortem and the Forensic report," Detective Sergeant Melbrook, as his name turned out to be, was saying. "And we are now sure that Ralph Pulleine was not pushed; he simply fell as the banisters gave way."

There was a silence, which George eventually felt obliged to break.

"Well, I could have told you that."

The detective remained impassive.

"Were you aware that the banisters on the second floor of the West Wing were rotting?"

"I was aware that the whole of the West Wing was rotting."

"So it didn't really come as a surprise to you when the accident happened."

"It came as a shock to me."

There was another pause. The second Detective did not appear to have anything to contribute. He sat silently throughout the proceeding, apparently taking it all in.

"I wouldn't have thought that you'd have anything in common, you and Ralph," went on Melbrook.

"We were different, certainly. That doesn't mean we didn't get on."

"You got on so well that Ralph left the Hall to you in his will," pronounced the Detective with emphasised diction.

"Yes. He felt sorry for me, I think." The Detective was staring at him professionally. George stared back and said nothing.

"You do realise that that probate for the will cannot be granted until after the inquest."

"Naturally," said George, folding his arms.

George was released that evening without charge. He was a little surprised that they had not kept him in for the full twenty-four hours – or was it forty-eight? George dared not leave the Hall; he felt that it would remain his as long as he stayed there; in any case, he had nowhere to go, apart from the flat, and he would soon be evicted from that. He just needed to get through the waiting period, which necessitated doing nothing at all. His only task for the present was to steer clear of the mother; he had not seen her since their last conversation in the morning room. This should be a simple matter as she appeared to be revolving around three areas; her suite of rooms, the drawing-room and the morning-room; there was no reason why he should ever need to go into these places, at least, not until the Hall was really his. It was only tension that was continuing to plague him, mentally and physically, a state which was entirely new to him.

CHAPTER 15

When George woke up on Monday, the twenty-fourth of April, 1995 in the guest room at Carshalton Hall, he remembered immediately that it was the morning of the inquest. The inquiry was to be held at 10 a.m. at the Coroner's Court in Darlington.

He slid out of bed and got ready very quickly. Through the windows, the sky appeared grey and uncompromising. Though as he came out onto the gravelled drive outside, there were signs that it would brighten up later.

As George travelled into town by bus, he felt cool, calm and collected. There was no need to be nervous or guarded – he could tell it exactly how it was – he was showing Ralph the secret passage, he had needed the toilet, he had gone to the toilet in the East Wing, he had returned to the West Wing hallway. Ralph had been up on the second floor and when George called out to him, and he must have leant over. He could even repeat the poor man's last words to him: Where are you, George? Are you downstairs? He would be telling the truth, an act which required no effort at all. So, standing in the courtroom, it was with a steady right hand that George held a black, hard backed copy of the King James version of the Bible and swore by Almighty God that he would tell the truth, the whole truth and nothing but the truth. Again, he did not have a lawyer present; why would an innocent bystander need a lawyer? The mother, however, had not waived this privilege. She was sitting in the front row of the benches, staring fixedly at him throughout the entire proceeding. Her counsel, a learned looking man who sat at a table close by, persisted in asking George the strangest of questions, not unlike those already posed to him down at the Custody Suite. But as they were not of a directly accusing nature, he was able to answer them truthfully as well. When the jury retired to deliberate, George decided to get some air. He walked hurriedly out of the courtroom, down the long corridors, past the security staff and down some stone steps leading to the pavement outside. He kept going and went into a pub a few streets down. But half an hour he was back again and found that a verdict had already been reached; a verdict of accidental death. George left the courtroom immediately and went straight home.

He was the first to arrive back at the Hall. Surely it was now his. No doubt the mother would make further attempts to block his legitimate progress, but would probably fail. His thoughts turned to more immediate matters such as the question of his name. Now, he felt was a good time to change it. Tomorrow he would find a solicitor in Darlington who would oblige. In a short time he would not be plain old George Alderson, but George Pulleine Esquire, of Carshalton Hall. Up in the guest room, in which he was still settled, he practiced writing his new signature. With flourishing strokes and a firm underline, he wrote it out several times, each time an improvement on the last. Finally he was satisfied; his new identity had been formulated in ink.

He thought he could hear the mother and Gertrude returning. Now was not a good time to go downstairs. The house seemed rather quiet without Ralph; in a way, he was almost missing him. But focussing again upon his new image, he put the dead young man out of his mind. Lying down on the bed, he contemplated upon what he might do for the rest of the day.

CHAPTER 16

It was the end of the summer. The long awaited letter from Ralph's solicitor had finally arrived. It lay at the breakfast table, between the toast rack and the newspaper, both of which were now provided by Gertrude, albeit reluctantly. As his eyes slid down the page, a great sense of importance and achievement began to overwhelm him. Carshalton Hall was finally his. The mother would have Right of Occupancy but could do nothing about his ownership status. George smiled the broadest smile that he had smiled for some time. When he wanted something, he usually got it.

Later that morning, filled with pride, he ambled along towards the West Wing.

As he passed through the familiar oak door which was the gateway between two worlds, a new sense of freedom and elation overcame him. Before, he had felt like some kind of stowaway. Now he was master and commander. As he reached the Divan Room, on the upper floor, he stared disapprovingly at the old, tacky wallpaper with which someone had taken it into their heads to decorate the room a hundred years ago; however that would soon be changed. He had already contacted experts from a building conservation trust, who had been very interested in taking samples of old wallpaper back with them for analysis. On confirmation that the house was legally his, they would be more than willing to strip the wallpaper back to the 1711 layer, in exchange for the outer layers. It had all been pre-arranged; they were just waiting for a word. His ultimate intention was to transform the entire West Wing into a time capsule from the year 1711. He continued to pass through room after room, marvelling at how the place would eventually look. Though the entire transformation would cost a fortune. George was not quite sure where the money would be coming from. Without a gentleman's income to go with the Hall, his movements were rather restricted.

The conservation team arrived within a fortnight. It consisted of two women: one with short dark hair and earrings who appeared to be the leader and the other wearing a white coat and with dark hair tied back. They were now in the Divan room; a ladder was extended near to one of the high walls and equipment scattered around. George stood watching them from the door as they soaked the outermost layer, wearing cotton gloves. "How old do you think the bottom layer will be?" George asked, after a while. He was a little afraid that wallpaper might not have existed in Catherine's day.

The woman with the earrings turned to face him.

"Oh, seventeenth or eighteenth century, possibly," she said. "It was very expensive to remove wallpaper in those days. Though I suppose the sort of people living here wouldn't have to worry about that."

"How many layers are there?"

"Could be twenty. At least fifteen, I'd say."

They had already begun to peel off the outermost layer, in swathes. Uninterested in the technicalities, George decided to leave them to their labours. He went back through the oak door and into the East Wing. As he hopped up the central stairway in his usual half-run, he was dismayed to see the mother in a grey dress suit, approaching from above. This was an unusual occurrence, for she rarely ventured upstairs. Stooped and wrinkled before her time, she was climbing down the stairs very slowly, with the aid of the stair rail and a stick. As they passed, she turned towards him and regarded him with a poisonous look. It had the desired effect. George felt acutely uncomfortable. He remembered that the woman was only sixty-seven and despite her aged appearance, she could potentially remain at Carshalton in an earthly state for at least another twenty years. There might be no getting rid of her. The thought was unbearable. He hurried up the remaining steps, trying to ignore her. On reaching the top, it occurred to him to wonder what she had been doing up there in the first place. Perhaps she had gone to look at Ralph's room.

In the late afternoon, George returned to the Divan Room, to see how the wallpaper experts were getting on. A section of the bottom layer was now visible. It was of a beautiful blue, floral design with stems and leaves in different shades curving around the patchy paper. Amidst these were shapes vaguely resembling Chinese birds.

"I'd say this was early 1700s," the short-haired woman was saying. "It's actually rather well preserved. Not too much staining. Quite a find, in fact."

"I want the whole room stripped back to that wallpaper," said George. They were knocking off now but would return at eight the following morning. "Can you stick down the bit at the top which seems to be lifting away from the wall?"

"Yes. We have a special paste for that."

George decided to assume that they knew what they were doing with the fragile eighteenth century wallpaper. It had presumably to be treated with the utmost care. But after they had left, he could not resist reaching out and touching it; it felt silky and delicate, not really like paper at all.

As George entered the Divan Room the following afternoon, his spirits soared; the experts had finished their task of stripping back the wallpaper. It was a revelation. From floor to ceiling, all four walls were covered in the blue floral design, perfectly matching the Turkish divan. True, it was a bit browned in places, but George considered it beautiful. The woman in the white coat appeared to be drying off one piece of it using nothing more than a common hairdryer. The other turned to face him with a slight smile.

"We can improve the appearance of the wallpaper significantly," she said, in a smooth tone. "The whole surface will have to be cleaned. We've removed the water stains from one small area already by spraying them with pieces of blotter soaked in water and ethanol. It's better to diffuse the stains rather than to directly remove them."

George was amazed at how much brighter the wallpaper looked in that place. It was almost as good as new. "Keep going," he instructed, continuing to look all around at the antique paper. On the east wall was a symmetrical patch, as though something manmade had covered it for many years. The shape seemed familiar, and a moment later, George realised why. The mirror with the scratches and gilded frame had been taken down and placed by the window during the course of the refurbishment. George walked over to it and lifted it by its sides; it was heavy and unwieldy; however he was able to carry it over to the other wall. Holding the mirror up, it concealed the patch exactly. He would reinstall it in its rightful place at the first opportunity.

Several days later, the work was complete. George signed a piece of paper to the effect that they might do as they like with the outer wallpaper samples. As soon as they had gone, he fetched plugs from the toolbox from the garage and fitted up the mirror. The glass was in two pieces; a horizontal line ran between them near the top.

Now the room was exactly as it had been in 1711. Of course, items of furniture other than the Turkish divan might have been present, but at least the basics were there. In the scarred glass of the mirror, George could see the field at the back of the house leading down to the beck. The blueness of the wallpaper in the room seemed bluer and the oak floorboards, lighter. George opened the windows and allowed the warm September air to pervade the room. As he wandered around its spacious interior, he felt just like an eighteenth century gentleman, which was of course, what George Alderson alias Pulen should have been. George made the decision never to sell Carshalton Hall.

CHAPTER 17

The servants were starting to seriously irritate George. They had irritated him from the start but now things were becoming intolerable. It was not so much that they were noisy or being a nuisance, it was just the knowledge that they were there. This was particularly annoying at night. The mother was well out of the way in her suite of rooms, but Gertrude was living close to him. When he had ordered her to move, she had refused. George wished that he could sack all the servants and replace them with a new lot. Unfortunately this was not possible. The servants apparently went with the mother and could stay as long as she did. However, they were serving a useful purpose. Housework was not something that George was inclined to get bogged down with. Finally George decided to sleep in the Victorian Ensuite guestroom with the green décor, situated in the West Wing. The plumbing there did not work, so he brought a bucket of water and placed it in the bathroom. For lighting, he used the white, wax candles that were always kept along with the tablecloths in a cupboard near the kitchen area. It was a bit dusty in the room; he would get Gertrude to spring-clean it.

One thing was bothering him; the wild mushrooms

that had accompanied the pheasant last night had tasted funny, and today he felt ever so slightly ill. It was an almost imperceptible feeling of malaise, but as George had never had a day's illness in his life, it was worrying. The next day the feeling grew stronger; the day after it was still more noticeable, and in addition, he was now experiencing mild stomach cramps and strange mood changes accompanied by lightheadedness. George took to taking his meals down at The Stanwick Arms. On one such occasion, as he sat at a corner table, eating, he considered for the first time the idea of selling Carshalton Hall. But, he reflected, the price would be drastically reduced by the sitting occupants. George admitted to himself that he was beginning to feel depressed. It was a continual, ongoing depression, unlike any temporary despondency that he had suffered in the past.

However, the following day, there was some good news. The application process for the memorial to Catherine Pulleine had gone through. George was a little surprised; at each stage, he had expected to be obstructed by some obstinate member of the clergy. In less than two weeks, a spanking new rhomboid memorial, complete with flower vase and candle-holders was erected on the North Wall of the church, close to that of Wingate Pulleine. George had never discovered a burial date for Catherine Pulleine. He was content to have inscribed the words:

In Memory of
Catherine Pulleine of Carshalton
Born c.1693

George was pleased. He now felt well and truly rooted at Carshalton Hall. Standing inside the church admiring it, he wondered for how many centuries the memorial would remain there. After examining it in detail, George decided to have a wander around the graveyard. He did a circuit of the church, walking past the north wall where the more recent Pulleines lay, noticing again with some degree of unease the single plot that appeared to be still available for another Pulleine. The stomach cramps and light-headedness were coming on again.

George's lifestyle was becoming increasingly similar to that of the late Ralph Pulleine. As each day passed, he was becoming ever lazier and ineffectual. There was the continual problem of what to do all day. Now that Ralph was gone, he had nobody to talk to, apart from the locals down the pub and they weren't the greatest of conversationalists. The servants also seemed to be standing against him, in his own home. However, he was determined not to let them drive him out. The stomach cramps, though still persistent, did not appear to be getting any worse. George did not go to doctors much, and he decided to wait and see if the symptoms would disappear on their own. Surely the mother or her servants could not be poisoning him? George was still suspicious of those mushrooms picked a week or so ago by Gertrude's fair hands. He was not an expert on mushrooms, so had looked up all the poisonous mushrooms in a book that he had found in the new library in the East Wing but could not find any mushrooms which resembled the ones which he had consumed that evening. George was not accustomed to anxiety neurosis; however, he did decide not to dine at Carshalton Hall anymore.

*

George was lying on the Turkish divan in the Divan
Room. His mood was not good. Having achieved his
ambition, life now seemed empty and worthless. It had
never occurred to him that he would ever become like
this after acquiring the Hall; he had envisaged only hap-
piness and fulfilment. He was trying not to fall asleep;
these days he often felt as though he was drugged up to
the eyeballs. At least the stomach cramps had eased off
for the moment.

He thought he could hear the sound of quick, approaching footsteps. As he turned his world-weary head
towards the door, he caught sight of Rose standing there,
dressed in new, ironed clothes. At first, she said nothing,
but then entered the room without invitation. George
remembered what the mother had been saying at the
dining table some months before and vaguely wondered
if that might have something to do with her visit. George
invited her to sit down, and she immediately took a seat
on the other part of the L-shaped divan. She appeared
plumper than how he remembered her. George regarded
her in an uninterested fashion.

"I was wondering if you would like to see your son,"
began Rose.

"My son?" echoed George, unapproachably.

"He is your son. And he needs a father."

How trite, thought George. Then the next bit came.

"I thought it would be much better for him to live
here."

There was a pause.

"There is no question of either you or him living here,"
pronounced George. "You'll just have to find a flat."

"I already have a flat," said Rose.

George remembered what the mother had said about finding Rose a flat. Knowing the parsimonious nature of the mother, George could imagine what sort of flat it would be. No wonder Rose was seeking alternative accommodation.

George sat up then leant on his forearms.

"Rose," he said. "I can't help you."

Rose did not appear able to answer. She looked upset and disturbed.

George stood up. "I'm about to go out," he said.

Rose also stood up. George viewed her with impatient expectation. As Rose walked away along the corridor, she did look round once at George, who stood at the door, watching her.

George's melancholia increased as the days turned slowly over, one after the other. He was now spending long periods of time leaning against the aged, oak panelling in the Gallery, staring wondrously up at the portrait of Catherine Pulleine. She had such an imaginative expression. It seemed to vary and fluctuate, depending on his current mood. Sometimes it seemed sarcastic and mischievous, other times, green and dreaming. On several occasions, when wandering about alone in the West Wing, or around the field and woodlands at the back of the house, he had thought he could sense her presence. And one afternoon whilst pottering around in the Divan Room at a time when he was feeling particularly light-headed, a strange and disturbing event had occurred. He had, as he often did, been gazing into the gold framed mirror with the black scratches and for a moment, thought he could see Catherine herself, reclining on the Turkish divan, clad in a purple gown, of the same tincture as the riding-dress in the portrait, her ash-blonde hair draped over the soft cushions. Then she was gone, and all he could see was the light blue covering on the divan. He began to question his psychological state. Perhaps it was not a doctor that he needed, but a psychiatrist.

One afternoon near the end of October when George was returning from the Post Office at Aldbrough he took the footpath across the fields towards Stanwick, intending to place wild flowers in the vase in Catherine Pulleine's memorial. Finally the illegitimate heir to the Pulleine estate had received his rightful inheritance. It was beginning to cloud over, and a few drops of rain fell. George was glad of the fresh, cool air. The last days had been unusually warm. No wonder his stomach cramps had affected him badly just recently. He was feeling better now. As he came down the other side of the hill, he glanced behind him. Up above was a herd of black cows with yellow tags in their ears. He could not remember seeing them there or anywhere else before. He carried on walking down the stony grass. Glancing towards the cows again he noticed that they were approaching him, en masse. George quickened his pace. He was not going to stand his ground with them. The black cows continued to follow him, but at the same steady pace. There was line of barbed wire at the edge of the field, and George got behind it. They wouldn't be following him over that. Soon he was over a stile and onto the main road.

Having reached the corner of the field, the black cows appeared to be stuck there and began grazing again. George wondered what would have happened if he had allowed them to reach him. Probably nothing, but he had been intimidated. He walked along the asphalted road until reaching a second stile, which took him into the field with a footpath leading along the beck to Stanwick Church. Here there were only harmless sheep. Eventually he reached the graveyard encircling the church.

When he reached the door of the church, the sun was approaching the horizon. It seemed remarkably low for four-thirty. Then in his clouded brain, it dawned on him that the clocks must have gone back the previous night.

The sombre interior of the church was deserted as usual. He began placing the wild flowers in the memorial vase. Then he took new candles from the altar. As he positioned them in their holders, he suddenly became vaguely aware that he was not alone. Turning around, he observed a man in his fifties or sixties dressed in ecclesiastical attire, seated in a nearby pew. George wondered what he was doing there. As if reading his thoughts, the Reverend spoke in a definite voice.

"There will be a service here in about an hour. I presume that you will attend."

George felt irritated. How dare this man presume things about the Lord of the Manor, as he now was. However, aristocrats were supposed to be polite, so he said,

"I didn't realize that the church was still in use for services," he said.

"There is a service whenever there is a fifth Sunday in the month," said the Reverend. There was a pause. Then

George confessed to being a non-believer, and in any case, he had to admit to not feeling very well. It was true, the stomach pains were getting quite a lot worse, now.

"Oh, such a shame, such a shame." The Reverend stood up. "I don't believe we've met. I am the Reverend Wendlebury. And I presume that you are George Alderson, the new owner of Carshalton Hall."

"George Pulleine," returned George, curtly.

"Yes, of course, of course. But I don't know if that's anything to be proud of. The Pulleines were a bad lot. Always double-dealing and double-crossing, clapping defenceless persons in prison. Many a poor peasant died as a result of their harsh treatment. Although I can say that their character is much improved of late." "Yes," said George.

"It was a terrible business, about young Ralph," went on the Reverend. "Such a tragic loss of life. I just can't understand it."

"No," agreed George.

The Reverend regarded him with gimlet eyes.

"And now you're the new owner of Carshalton Hall. Well, Ralph's misfortune is your fortune."

George did not like the road that the Reverend appeared to be going down. He decided to leave. As he walked away down the aisle, the Reverend called out to him:

"May the Lord forgive you for all your sins and have mercy on your soul."

Pompous ass, thought George. He wished he had the power to sack vicars. Come to think of it, he really didn't have any power at all.

The evening sky was becoming overcast, and a few

drops of rain fell. The stomach cramps were coming on again, more so than ever before. Perhaps he should go to a doctor after all. He resolved to do this tomorrow. He just did not know what was wrong with him. Surely the mother could not still be poisoning him. He did not seriously believe that she was. Nor did he think that any of her remaining servants were responsible. He had not eaten at Carshalton for over a month. In any case, he couldn't eat anything tonight, with his stomach in the state it was in.

When George got back to Carshalton Hall, the rain was starting to come down heavily, and he was relieved to get inside. He went straight to his Victorian bed chamber and collapsed immediately upon the covers of the four-poster bed. Within minutes he was asleep; a slumber which became deeper as the hours passed, a general slowing down of his bodily functions until, just after three in the morning, they stopped altogether, pronouncing his physical death. Two mornings later, George was discovered by Gertrude lying dead in the four-poster bed, in a suitably poetic pose. She was instantly shocked by his deathly pallor, which caused her to cry out and run back through the rooms of the Hall.

A week later Lady Pulleine sat in the morning room, reading the Yorkshire Post. This was not a circulation to which she would normally turn her attention. However within this particular edition ran an article relating to her own good self:

'A bizarre case of arsenic poisoning occurred last week, leading to the death of George Pulleine, 31, recent acquirer of Carshalton Hall, Carshalton, in the parish of Stanwick-St-John. Traces of arsenic were found in the deceased man's hair, and these were quickly ascertained to have come from a dye used in the wallpaper, known during the nineteenth century as Emerald Green, or Paris Green. Fungus living on the wallpaper paste re-acted with the dye to produce arsine gas, which the dead man had inhaled whilst sleeping.

Arsenic poisoning from wallpaper caused countless deaths during the Victorian era, and the dyes responsible were phased out only as late as the twentieth century. Examples of wallpaper containing the dye include those designed by William Morris, such as his *trellis* design, (See photograph). The most famous case of suspected arsenic poisoning from wallpaper was the death of Napoleon Buonaparte, though this was never confirmed. The arsenic dyes were used not only in wallpapers but also in food and clothing.

George Pulleine will be laid to rest in the church of Stanwick-St-John, alongside his ancestors in the Pulleine family plot.'

Lady Pulleine lowered the newspaper. She had heard nothing of this final statement. Was it right that her son's murderer should be buried amongst her husband's kins-folk? She decided that it was. She wanted him kept where she could see him, damn him and curse him. Though it was really herself whom she wished to damn and curse. It was her own fault that her son was dead. Consumed by guilt, she was starting to become completely withdrawn and would speak to no one. Her thoughts had become a perpetual series of 'if onlys' and 'should haves'. In the midst of all her self-destructive analysis, an aspect of her son's persona had recently struck her. Ralph had never had a girlfriend. Was it possible that he was effeminate? Was that why he had never desired to make money? The more she thought about it, the more reasonable the idea seemed. If only she had realised earlier. No doubt the perversion was also her fault.

Gertrude came into the morning room to collect the tea-tray. Unusually, there had been a second post that day, and she proffered an official looking letter awaiting the attention of her employer.

"Please open it and read it to me, Gertrude," whispered Lady Pulleine.

Gertrude put down the tea-tray. She picked up the letter knife lying on the corner table beside the armchair, flipped open the envelope and took out the thick, parchment paper within.

"It's from Rose's solicitors," she said. Lady Pulleine said nothing.

Gertrude began to read in her clear, cool voice.

'Dear Lady Pulleine

I am writing to inform you that Carshalton Hall is now held in trust for George Stokes, son of the late George Pulleine of Carshalton Hall and Rose Hippolita Stokes. I believe, however, that you hold right of occupancy and shall continue to do so until your death.

Ms Stokes has informed me that she would like her son and herself to take up residence at Carshalton Hall ...'

Gertrude stopped reading and glanced at her employer. But the afflicted woman appeared to be in a world of her own. She put the letter down on the occasional table and carried the tea-tray out of the room.